PARAMOUNT (Columbia) PICTURES *presents*

A John Heyman-Burtt Harris Production

MARY BETH HURT

MICHAEL McKEAN

KATHRYN WALKER

COLLEEN CAMP

JOSEF SOMMER

and **BARRET OLIVER** as Daryl

Co-produced by
Burtt Harris *and* **Gabrielle Kelly**

Written by
David Ambrose & **Allan Scott** *and* **Jeffrey Ellis**

Produced by
John Heyman

Directed by
Simon Wincer

D.A.R.Y.L.

adapted by **N. H. KLEINBAUM**

from a screenplay written by

DAVID AMBROSE & ALLAN SCOTT
and **JEFFREY ELLIS**

Pacer BOOKS FOR YOUNG ADULTS

a member of The Putnam Publishing Group
New York

Pacer Books are published by
The Putnam Young Readers Group
51 Madison Avenue
New York, New York 10010

ISBN: 0-425-08432-9
Pacer is a trademark belonging to
The Putnam Publishing Group.
The name "BERKLEY" and the stylized "B"
with design are trademarks belonging
to Berkley Publishing Corporation.

Printed in the United States of America
First Printing July 1985

.1.

The majesty of the snow-capped mountains dwarfed the swiftly moving red Buick which sped along the narrow winding highway. The air was still. Only the sound of the car's engine racing along intruded on the silence. The sleek car zigzagged in and out of sharp turns, lurching at breakneck speed deeper into the mountain range.

A ten-year-old boy gripped the backseat of the speeding vehicle as he peered out the windows at the mighty Appalachian mountains that loomed above him against the gray winter sky. "They must have been here forever," he said to himself. He hunched farther down into the rear seat, shifted his eyes and gazed intently at the man who was driving.

In the front seat Mulligan steered the speeding

vehicle around a knife-edged curve. He held his breath as the car came dangerously close to the edge. When they cleared the bend, Mulligan turned to the boy in the back. "So far, so good, Daryl," he said smiling weakly, unable to hide his fear. Mulligan thought he could almost feel the boy's fear merge with his own. The boy watched silently, his wide-set, penetrating eyes focused intently on Mulligan. For a moment Mulligan caught Daryl's face in the mirror. The boy looked average for his ten years, plain features, a thatch of dark hair, slender, intense and intelligent. Daryl looked almost ordinary.

Roadside trees whipped their shadows, coming frighteningly close as Mulligan accelerated the car as fast as it could go. The silent tension mounted as the speed increased. The tires hardly touched the asphalt below. Without warning, the car crested a hill.

Nearby, deep in the woods of the Appalachians, Mattie and Mabel Bergen climbed into their old truck after a day of squirrel hunting. They had had a good day, with seven squirrels as their prize ... but they were tired and anxious to head for home. Mabel sat back in the cab of the pickup as her husband released the brake and the old four-wheeler rolled forward. He rammed it into gear and brought the engine sputtering to life. Just before his own engine fired, he heard the sound of a car somewhere nearby.

As his truck nosed onto the firebreak road, he

spotted the red Buick a hundred feet away, racing at breakneck speed directly toward his truck. "Oh my God," Mabel screamed, "he's going to hit us!" The old man wrenched his wheel and slid the truck into the shoulder rut. Mabel uncovered her eyes as the red car thundered past and disappeared up the track. Suddenly, a deafening sound shattered the silence of the mountainside.

"Oh my God," Mable squealed. "What was that?"

At the same instant, a helicopter had swooped over the ledge of the cliff, just inches above ground level, heading straight for the Buick.

Inside the car, Mulligan and Daryl roared on the seemingly endless road. Suddenly they faced a wall of boulders which had been shoved across the roadway, barring the sheer, deadly precipice drop beyond. The Buick rattled over and between the boulders soaring outward and plummeted three hundred feet to obliteration. The car smashed and burst into flames. It had been reduced to a red fireball, blazing intensely, poised to plunge an additional hundred feet to the river below.

Hearing the crash and seeing the rising flames from the explosion, Bergen and his wife stared off into the distance. "We'd better go see...," Mabel began. They looked helplessly towards the corner where the car had disappeared.

As they climbed back into the truck to investigate the crash, they heard a sound, faint and weak. Mabel Bergen stumbled from the truck, searching through the underbrush. She pushed through the

7

woods in a frantic search—the sound seemed to be a child's cry for help. She rushed closer and closer to the faint, tentative sound. Her husband set the hand brake and climbed slowly out of the truck, still shaking his head in wonder. He followed his wife's trail through the woods.

Suddenly the old woman spotted the grimy-faced, soot-covered body. Daryl lay sprawled on the ground. His entire body flinched as Mrs. Bergen reached out a hand. "It's okay, sonny, you're all right now, ain't ya?" the white-haired woman asked a wide-eyed Daryl. "Mabel's here now, sonny. We'll look after ya now." Daryl remained still, baffled, silent. Suddenly, Old Man Bergen looked through the underbrush, his piercing eyes and half-shaven face frightening the child even more.

"Easy, Mattie," the old woman said to her husband. "He's real skeered...and he..." Mabel was startled when Daryl just let himself relax in her unfamiliar arms. She cradled him lovingly. "Just like when Amos was little, ain't he...?" she said to her husband. "We could raise him, Mattie..."

"You can't just take on a child because you found him," Bergen answered, watching his wife's face glow with a joy he hadn't seen in a long time.

"Mebbe," she said. "We'll get him well first, though."

As the Bergens moved with Daryl toward the truck, the burning wreckage took its final plunge, tumbling, with Mulligan, from the ledge. The pieces

8

slithered into the water and were swept downward in the rapid current.

Up above, the helicopter returned to sweep over the surface of the river. Men in dark glasses peered intently, as if trying to track the fragments or locate any bodily remains. Bergen lifted Daryl gently to his feet and the trio started to walk from the woods. After a few steps, Mrs. Bergen crouched beside the solemn, silent child who had not shed a tear, and put her hands on his shoulders.

"What's your name, sonny, hmmm?" she asked.

"My name is Daryl."

"An' what you doin' up in these parts?" she pressed.

"I don't know," he said calmly.

They neared the truck and all three climbed into the front cab, Daryl squeezed between the strangers who'd rescued him. The old man started up the engine, and they headed out of the woods and onto the roadway.

.2.

Mr. Bergen called Daryl into their run-down living room. Bergen's hair seemed whiter, dark circles around his piercing eyes. He'd never been much at conversation, but he began his speech to Daryl.

"Can't believe Mabel is gone," the old man confided to the boy. Daryl had been living with the couple just a few short weeks. "That bug just grabbed her. Her heart wasn't great; the doc had told me that but..." A tear trickled down the craggy old face.

"Trouble is," he looked intently at the sad-faced child, "with Mabel gone, I jest cain't keep ya. Ya know what I mean? They'll find a place for ya. You'll be okay."

Daryl stared back silently. There was nothing he could say.

□ □ □

Bergen and Daryl climbed into the rickety old pickup and headed to Gartonville. The old man and the boy drove silently into town until the truck lurched to a stop on Main Street.

"Wait here," Bergen instructed Daryl, as he got out of the truck and walked slowly into the government administration building, hitching up his pants as he neared the door.

Old Man Bergen looked around the small room where city business took place. He felt uncomfortable as he glanced at the different signs, trying to decide where to go.

"Need any help?" asked the woman behind the desk in the entranceway.

"Got to report a death," he said flatly.

"Over here," she gestured, pulling down a book and opening it.

"Relative?" Mrs. Gough asked.

"My wife," Bergan said simply.

"And when was this?"

"About two, three weeks back. But it's the boy I gotta have took care of, see..."

"And who certified the death?" Mrs. Gough asked.

"Who what?" Bergen asked.

Outside, Daryl jumped down from the truck and crossed to watch some children playing behind the fence of a small schoolyard. A heated fight broke out on the basketball court. One of the boys turned and asked Daryl, "You saw it, didn't ya?"

"I'm sorry?" Daryl looked back, confused.

"Was it a foul or wasn't it?"

"I don't, uh... I'm sorry...," Daryl stammered.

"Don't you know anything?" a second boy asked in disbelief.

Daryl stood facing the eight angry children and began to back away cautiously. Turning toward the truck, he sprinted and locked himself inside. The kids watched him for a moment, puzzled.

"Weird," one boy said, shaking his head.

"You ain't kiddin'," his pal agreed, walking back to the game.

Mr. Bergen walked out of the building and waved to Daryl to join him on the sidewalk.

"The lady here has arranged for you to go to a children's home," Bergen said gently. "They'll take care of you better'n I could do. I'm sorry about this, boy. Now follow this here nice lady," and he pointed Daryl in the right direction.

Bergen stuck out his callused old hand. Daryl reached out and shook hands solemnly. Bergen affectionately stroked Daryl's cheek and warned him, "Now you be good, hear? And God bless."

He turned and walked toward the pickup truck. In a moment he was gone.

.3.

"Can you read the letters up on the board over there?" asked the doctor at the Barkenton Child Care Facility.

Daryl glanced at the chart hanging on the door, then looked at the doctor and repeated, "Q, Z, R, T, U, S, F, E, J, K, C, W, Y, M, G, T, R, U, P, A, V, B."

The doctor looked from Daryl to the chart, and back to Daryl again. Surprised at what he had just witnessed, he asked Daryl to read the letters one more time. When Daryl proceeded to do so in exactly the same fashion, the doctor stopped him and walked over to a desk full of papers. He marked up a legal pad, stared out the window, then continued writing. Occasionally he cast a glance at Daryl with knitted brows.

After the examination, Daryl was taken to meet the director of the facility, Howie Fox.

"Glad to meet you, Daryl. Welcome aboard!" Howie ushered Daryl across the yard where a group of kids were playing volleyball.

"Daryl, I'd like you to meet my wife, Elaine." Howie smiled as he introduced his wife.

"Hiya, Daryl." Elaine smiled and patted Daryl on the head.

"Hello, Elaine, it's nice to meet you," Daryl replied politely.

Howie and Daryl continued across the campus, entered one of the buildings and went into an office.

"One thing you can be sure of, Daryl," Howie said trying to reassure him, "somewhere somebody is looking for you. And we'll hear from them."

Daryl regarded him solemnly, without answering.

"Until then, we're just going to make you as comfortable as we can."

A knock at the door interrupted them, and the doctor who had examined Daryl strutted in and placed a folder on the table.

"Physically, he's one hundred percent. But he is suffering from substantial amnesia. He doesn't remember his parents, his home or anything like that. My guess is it's psychological rather than structural memory loss. He's handling himself alright."

Howie picked up the folder and thumbed through some of the pages. He crouched down in front of

Daryl so as to be at eye level when he spoke.

"You're going to be spending a few nights here, Daryl, until we can find a family to look after you. Once your folks show up, they can take you home."

Daryl looked directly at Howie. "Thank you," he said, "it is extremely kind of you to be looking after my welfare like this."

Howie shot the doctor a quizzical look. Both were taken aback by Daryl's formality.

Howie shrugged awkwardly and said, "Yeah, well, that's what we do here."

Howie parked his car across the street from a large construction site.

"It's getting there," Howie grinned at Andy Richardson as he stepped back to regard the huge operation.

"Some people gotta work for a living, not like some guys I know," Andy laughed. He took off his hard hat and wiped his sweaty brow with a soiled handkerchief. "How was the vacation?"

"Terrific," Howie said, but he quickly dismissed the subject.

"Listen, Andy, there's something I have to talk to you about. It's not exactly the way we hoped it would be, but... You got a minute?"

Andy ran up the porch stairs. He threw open the door and almost knocked over the small girl who was reaching for the knob. "Sorry," Andy said rapidly as he brushed by the girl to find his wife, Joyce.

"Last one?" Andy asked Joyce as her piano student ran down the walk.

"Yes, why?" Joyce asked as she kissed him and waited expectantly.

"Howie just came by the site. He had a question for us. They have a kid at the center. A boy, nine or ten..."

Joyce looked up at Andy and then turned away.

"They need a foster home while they try and find his family," Andy continued, "and Howie was wondering if we could help out."

"Well, that's what we're registered for, isn't it?" Joyce asked, her voice quivering slightly.

"Look, before we make any hasty decisions, let me tell you that he's suffered a loss of memory. So, if you have any doubts..." Andy paused.

"There's no chance of adopting a child if we don't foster one first," Joyce declared.

"Right now, all Howie is asking is for us to look after this little boy for a few days."

"Of course we'll look after him!" Joyce smiled, feeling more hopeful. Maybe her prayers had finally been answered. Maybe Joyce would finally have a child.

Howie's car pulled into the Richardson's driveway. Joyce heard the car doors slam and went to look out the window. She saw Howie and a small, dark-haired boy walk up to the house. She greeted them at the kitchen door.

"Come in, come in," Joyce said smiling. "We've been waiting for you. We're so glad you're here."

Joyce led Daryl to a table set with a glass of milk and a plate of cookies.

"What's your name?" Joyce asked, trying to break the ice.

"My name is Daryl. Thank you for the cookies, they look delicious."

Joyce felt at once that she wanted to hug him, but she held back. He looked so small and vulnerable. She wanted to mother him, but she didn't want to make Daryl feel uncomfortable by being too eager to welcome him into her home. Instead she knelt down beside him and gently put her arm on his shoulder.

"We're really glad you're here," she said again.

Daryl put down the cookie he was eating and politely said, "Thank you, Mrs. Richardson."

"Please, call me Joyce. And this is Andy," Joyce held out her hand for Andy to come join her. Andy walked up to Joyce and took her hand in his.

Daryl looked from Joyce to Andy and repeated "Joyce" and "Andy" as if memorizing their names and faces.

"It's great to have you here, Daryl. Howie's told us so much about you." Andy smiled.

"Come on, let's show Daryl around," Joyce suggested.

As they climbed the stairs, Andy picked up a baseball lying on the landing. "Hey Daryl, did you know that I'm the coach for the local Little League?" Andy tossed the ball to Daryl.

Daryl didn't even make an attempt to catch the ball. It hit off his chest and bounced down the stairs. Andy tried to cover up what he thought must have been an embarrassing moment for Daryl. "Caught you by surprise, huh? We can play catch later." But Daryl just stared at the ball as it rolled across the floor. He looked confused.

"Enough time for that," Joyce reprimanded Andy. Tightening her grip on Daryl, she led him up the stairs, as they heard Howie yell from the first floor that he'd show himself out.

.4.

The morning sun streamed in through the windows of the Richardson's bright kitchen. Joyce looked toward the door and smiled at the sight of her neighbor's child, his face pressed flat against the screen door.

"Hi, Turtle," she called, waving the boy in. "How was your vacation? I didn't get all the details from your mom and dad yet."

"It was okay. Only I discovered something more interesting than the vacation."

"What was that?" Joyce asked.

"Watching paint dry. Or cutting worms in half and watching both sexes wriggle."

Joyce smiled.

"So where's this famous kid you got?"

"Famous kid?"

"My dad says he's real cute." Turtle grimaced. "I think it's envy. I keep pointing out to him that he has a hundred percent boy of his own, namely me, Turtle Fox, right here!"

"Daryl's upstairs. I'll get him.

"Daryl! Daryl, honey. Come on down. I want you to meet somebody," Joyce called.

"Hold it," Turtle said. "I heard he doesn't remember where he's from or . . . I mean, is he . . . you know . . . soft in the head?" He waved his hands in the air and pointed to his head, making circles with his finger.

"No," Joyce said, making a face. "He isn't, and its not a subject you should discuss with him. Okay?"

"Oh, okay."

"Promise. The subject of his memory loss is *out*. Deal?"

"Scout's honor," Turtle agreed.

Just then Daryl entered the kitchen.

"Hi, you must be Daryl. I'm Turtle."

"Hello, Turtle," Daryl responded formally.

"Hey, listen, uh, Daryl, you want to take a walk with me to the park, or something?"

"That's a great idea," Joyce smiled. "I'd like you boys to become friends. Turtle's parents have been our dearest friends for years," she explained to Daryl.

Daryl nodded his head in agreement and the two walked out the screen door and into the street.

" . . . This is one of my newest projects," Turtle was saying, explaining why he needed to walk to the park. They stopped at a house on the way, and Turtle took a huge boxer that was tied by its leash to the front porch railing. "I'm into making money. So every week I walk Joey," he explained, pointing to the huge, overzealous dog. "This monster is Joey."

As soon as the boys reached the park, Turtle found a shady tree and tied the boxer to the trunk. He motioned Daryl to sit down beside him.

"Here," he offered, "have a stick of gum." Daryl took the gum and put it in his mouth as Turtle stared at him.

"I don't get it. You remember how to read, you remember you name, stuff like that, but you don't remember your family, your school, if you've got brothers and sisters ... it doesn't make sense." Turtle shook his head, bewildered.

"The doctor said maybe my memory could come back suddenly. Only no one really knows," Daryl replied.

Turtle looked at his watch and jumped up suddenly. "Hey, we better get back," he shouted. "You want to come back to my house? If we're real nice to her, maybe Hookie will let us play with her new computer."

"Okay. Who's Hookie?" Daryl asked.

"My sister, Sherie Lee." Turtle chuckled as he untied the dog, which started to go berserk when freed from the tree. He handed the leash to Daryl for their walk back through the park toward their houses.

"Hookie?" Daryl asked.

"Amateur hooker. She dates *every* night. I invented the name. It really pisses her off." Turtle laughed.

They crossed the park, Turtle running to keep up as the dog dragged Daryl along.

"What's a hooker?" Daryl asked.

The question was drowned out by the dog's noisy barking as Turtle took the leash from Daryl and marched the boxer up to a plump woman who was sunning herself in her front yard.

"Did Joey have a good run?" the woman asked as she took the leash from Turtle. "Got some air into Joey's lungs, did he?"

"He must have done ten miles today, Miss Kent," Turtle said with a straight face.

"Same time Tuesday, don't forget," Miss Kent said, handing Turtle a dollar bill. "Joey gets all excited when he knows it's your day for exercising him, Turtle."

The two boys strolled down the street, Turtle tucking his dollar into his money belt. Just then a station wagon pulled alongside the boys and Joyce leaned out.

"You want a ride?"

The two of them jumped into the car, which accelerated, turned at the end of the street and pulled up outside a rambling old house on the corner.

As they clambered out of the car, Turtle looked at Joyce briefly.

"I guess that's pretty fancy—driving half a block on a nice day!"

"Smartass," she laughed back. "I've just picked up your mother's rug from the cleaners."

She opened the trunk and gestured that she needed help. Daryl was instantly at her side and offered to help. Turtle moved a little slower.

Turtle's mother, Elaine, watched her son from the porch. "Move it, junior," she called.

Turtle moved into action at his mother's command, hauling the rolled-up rug into the house. With a glance of resentment, Turtle gestured at his mother for Daryl's benefit.

"Daryl, this is my mom."

"We met already. Hi again, Daryl. It's nice to see you here."

"Thank you, ma'am. But the pleasure is mine."

Turtle froze in horror and surprise at his new friend's formal response.

As Daryl and Turtle struggled to get the rug up the porch steps and into the house, Elaine and Joyce exchanged greetings. Elaine then had the boys maneuver the rug so that it could be hooked to a runner which would eventually position it draped on the wall.

Turtle was still in shock over Daryl's remark. "Listen, buddy," he said, "someday I'll explain to you how a guy can come off like a creep."

"That's enough, Turtle," Elaine interrupted. "You watch your mouth."

Joyce pulled on the cord and watched the rug rise into its place as the featured item in the hallway.

25

Turtle signaled to Daryl. "Let's go see if Hookie is upstairs."

Overhearing the invitation, Elaine yelled, "Will you *stop* with this Hookie business!" She added more kindly, "Daryl, treat our house like your own, uh, like Joyce and Andy's."

Turtle tugged at Daryl to force him upstairs and steered him in the direction of Sherie Lee's room. Turtle immediately headed for the computer and began playing the video game Pole Position. Sherie Lee made no comment as the boys entered her room, obviously accustomed to such intrusions by her brother. Turtle and Daryl were completely riveted to the action on the screen when Sherie Lee spoke.

"So Daryl, how come you can remember your name if you can't remember anything else?"

"You're boring us, twerp," Turtle said to his sister, without pausing in the game.

"I can bore anyone I like in *my* room," she countered. "That's the price you have to pay for coming into *my* room and using *my* computer."

Turning to face Sherie Lee, Daryl politely explained, "Amnesia is selective, which means that there is always partial memory. For example, I haven't forgotten how to speak."

Daryl's explanation seemed to satisfy Sherie Lee for the moment. Both of them turned to Turtle as he let out a groan.

"You struck out, stupid," Sherie Lee sneered as her brother lost a round with the computer.

"Forty-eight hundred, Hookie. Show me your best

score!" Hitting a control sequence, Turtle looked defiantly at his sister as BEST SCORE came up on the screen.

Watching the two argue, Daryl asked, "Could I have a try?"

"I'll have to show you how," Turtle answered.

"Hey, twerp," Sherie Lee cut in, "let him try. Joyce says he's so smart. Let him prove it."

"I think I understand," Daryl said as he sat down in front of the computer. He began the game, slowly but without error, as Turtle and his sister made faces at one another across the room.

In minutes, Daryl was traveling as fast as Turtle was driving when he crashed. The track was moving so fast, it was hard to make out the details.

Suddenly interested in what Daryl was doing, Sherie Lee and Turtle stopped their teasing and watched the computer screen in amazement.

The game had accelerated beyond all possibility of response. The track was literally a moving blur of speed. Yet Daryl continued to clock up points, weaving his car between the onrushing stream of vehicles hurtling in the other direction. The computer screen was howling. Turtle and Sherie Lee, totally captivated, were yelling encouragement at this phenomenon as Daryl accelerated the game even faster.

"Honestly, he's a great kid! You know more about this than I do. Should I nag him a bit?" Joyce asked her friend as they sat in Elaine's kitchen.

"Never stop nagging," Elaine stressed. "They think you don't love them if you don't nag."

"But how do you know you're not nagging too much?" Joyce asked.

"It's the kind of thing you get used to. Give yourself time. It's only natural for you to feel a little strange."

The two turned at the sound of Howie's car pulling into the driveway. Joyce stood by the window, looking out, suddenly thoughtful. "Elaine," she mused, "there must be somebody out there looking for Daryl."

Up in Sherie Lee's room Daryl beamed with pleasure at finishing his first game of Pole Position. Turtle and Sherie Lee turned to Daryl in silence and stared at him.

"That's a fun game!"

Turtle, in shock over what he had just seen, finally clutched Daryl's shoulder in silent tribute. His face was a picture of delight and astonishment.

Sherie Lee broke the silence. "You swear...you never played this before?"

"I don't think so." Daryl smiled.

"Right. But for all you know, you could have *invented* Pole Position."

"Aw, come on Hookie. He's only..."

"Will you stop calling me that!"

Daryl looked at Sherie Lee, who was pink-faced with anger, and turned to Turtle. "It seems to annoy your mother, too," he observed.

"Of course it does! That's the whole point!" Turtle shouted.

"I don't understand why you want to annoy your family," Daryl said with a quizzical look on his face.

"For a genius, you can be real stupid," Turtle groaned, turning to leave. Daryl began to go after him, then turned to Sherie Lee.

"What *is* a hooker?" he asked.

At the mention of the word, Sherie Lee screamed and started throwing a pile of magazines at Daryl. He ran from the room and down the stairs.

The boys were running out of the house as Howie approached from the carport.

"Hi, Dad!"

"Hi, guys!"

"Hello, Mr. Fox."

Howie turned to Daryl. "How's it going, Daryl? This kid of mine showing you all around all right?"

"Yes, thank you, Mr. Fox. Turtle and Hook... Sherie Lee have been very kind."

"Hey Dad, he is just the greatest ever at Pole Position! I would say, at a conservative estimate, world champion!"

Howie smiled at the boys as they ran off together.

.5.

Joyce's car—sporting a bumper sticker that read IF
YOU DON'T LIKE THE WAY I DRIVE, GET THE HELL OFF
THE SIDEWALK—screeched to a halt by the main
school gates. She drove up on the curb and cut the
engine. All the doors flew open and Turtle, Daryl
and two other children climbed out of the car. Joyce
was the last one to get out and she joined up with
Daryl who was waiting for her.

"It's okay, Joyce, I'll take him to registration,"
Turtle said outside the gate.

"Well, I think Daryl might like it better if I..."
Joyce hesitated.

"Nobody wants to show up with their mother on
their first day of school," Turtle said, rolling his
eyes.

Joyce turned to Daryl. "Daryl?"

"I appreciate your concern, Joyce. But I'm sure Turtle can show me where to register."

Joyce turned away to hide her hurt feelings. She so desperately wanted to go in with Daryl like a real mother. Daryl moved closer for a kiss good-bye. Moist-eyed, Joyce kissed him on the cheek and watched him go.

By that afternoon Daryl had already adapted to the school routine. Math class was a horror. Mr. Nesbitt caught timid Trudi Johnson cheating on a pop quiz. Glowering over Trudi, Nesbitt bellowed, "Do you know how much I despise cheating?" He repeated the question, forcing Trudi to shake her head in response. "Well," Nesbitt continued, "just imagine life without hope of ever getting back in my favor!"

Trudi sank down in her seat and tried to explain, "I only asked Andrea if she could..."

"Silence!" roared Nesbitt, his eyes twitching faster and faster as his anger rose. "This girl showed you how to work the problem. On a test, this is called 'cheating.' Now I can rightly call you a cheat, a despicable cheat."

Trudi's lower lip started to quiver and tears welled up in her eyes. The entire classroom was silent. Andrea, who sat nearby, caught Daryl's eye and winked at him, including him in this conspiracy. Daryl stared at her. She winked again. Smiling, he winked back.

James Frost noticed the exchange between Daryl and Andrea. Jealous that he wasn't getting any of Andrea's attention, he tried to move in on the action. But when his attempt to get Andrea's attention went unnoticed, he became furious. After all, he was James Frost—the strongest kid in his grade. He decided then and there that Daryl would be his next target.

Clearing his throat, Nesbitt called for the class's attention. "I will pretend this didn't happen. But if it ever happens again ..." The untold threat was left hanging in the air. Daryl peered around the classroom and Trudi caught his eye. She winked at him in the hope of finding a sympathetic friend. Daryl winked back and Trudi smiled.

The quiz was to be corrected in class today. "Pass your papers two places to your left," Mr. Nesbitt ordered. Daryl and Turtle were sitting together near the back of the room. Daryl reached for a quiz to correct. He whistled through it, ticking and crossing out, and within seconds he had corrected the whole test.

James Frost, still angry, watched as Daryl worked on the paper. Coughing and hissing, James finally drew the teacher's attention so that Nesbitt looked over and saw Daryl working away.

"Hey you, yes, you!" Nesbitt shouted. He scuttled between the row of desks and stood towering over Daryl. "What do you think you're doing? Changing the answers? Writing on somebody else's paper?" he yelled.

Daryl looked up calmly. "I was checking it, as you asked."

"But I haven't given you the answers yet!"

Daryl held the test sheet up to Nesbitt, who was now twitching wildly. Daryl smiled in recognition of this twitch and twitched back at the teacher.

"You'll find they're correctly checked. I've marked number 9 as right although, in fact, there is an error in the eighth decimal place...but only a calculus system could show that..." Nesbitt stared at the page and went silent. Slamming the paper down, he stalked away.

Turtle was beside himself with glee. Daryl had triumphed over the mean Mr. Nesbitt, but for James Frost, this was the last straw.

"New kid," Frost snarled to Murphy, "thinks he's real smart. Ain't smart enough to know how a new kid should behave." Another threat hung in the air.

Andy Richardson threw the baseball up in the air, patiently waiting for Turtle to help Daryl get his hand in the mitt. The sound of piano music drifted through the open living room window of the Richardson house. Joyce's voice could occasionally be heard instructing her pupil how to hold her hands and play a piece.

"Okay," Andy began, "now the main thing to remember is that baseball is the essence of all life in the universe. There is no fooling around when it comes to playing ball; this is a very, very serious game. If I hear so much as a giggle from either of you, we'll play a game called 'waxing the car.'" Turtle glanced at Daryl and chuckled.

Andy handed Daryl the bat and positioned him at the plate. "Now bend a little more at the waist, and spread your legs." Daryl straddled his legs so far apart that he lost balance and stumbled forward.

"No, no, no..." Andy laughed. "Not that far apart!"

Once Daryl was positioned correctly, Andy trotted out to the patch of dirt that he told Daryl was called "the pitcher's mound." "Okay, Daryl. Now relax and keep your eye on the ball." Andy wound his arm up and lifted his leg. Daryl thought this was all very strange, but he kept his eye on the ball anyway. Andy tossed a slow pitch. Daryl swung at the ball, connected and dropped the bat with a yelp of pain. The ball traveled over Andy's head and Turtle went to retrieve it as Andy made his way over to Daryl.

"I'm sorry, Daryl. I forgot to tell you to grip the bat firmly," Andy said, demonstrating how to grip a bat. As Andy placed his hands over the red masking tape grip, he reassured Daryl that he'd get it yet. "Daryl, you're a born major leaguer. I can tell, it's all in the eyes. Now this time keep a good grip, an easy stroke, and smack the ball right to Interstate 95. Okay!"

"I'll try," Daryl said feebly.

As Andy made his way back to the mound, Daryl

flexed and wiggled in a foolish attempt to loosen up. He bent his knees and extended his arms, his eyes narrowed in concentration.

Sensing that he was ready, Andy pitched the ball. The ball curved toward Daryl. As if in slow motion, the bat stroked with easy precision to meet it. The ball flattened and spread at the moment of contact, then sprung back into shape and soared off into the sky...

Andy and Turtle watched with gaping mouths as the ball left the vacant lot and disappeared over the Richardson's rooftop.

Daryl sauntered up to Andy. "Was that all right?"

Andy was so astonished he could hardly speak. "Let's do it one more time," Andy managed to get out. He quickly turned to Turtle and added, "Turtle, you're sworn to secrecy, hear?" Andy clapped his hands and shouted, "Once more around, Daryl, let's go."

Andy scooped up the ball and pitched a dipper. Daryl swung in for another effortless home run.

"Turtle...Daryl!!!!!" Andy couldn't believe his luck! He motioned for the boys to run in, and as he grabbed them around the shoulders, the trio shared a bear hug. While still huddled close together, Andy clapped Daryl on the back and called him his secret weapon for the upcoming baseball season.

"Daryl," Andy cheered, "you're a natural...a genius!"

"The Warriors!" Turtle exclaimed.

"We'll murder them!" Andy agreed. "Only nobody must know. None of us says anything about it..."

"About what?" Daryl asked, looking perplexed.

"About what, he asks. Don't you just love the kid, Turtle? He's modest, he's awesome! I have to be dreaming. Just one more pitch and then I'll wake up."

They all took their positions, Daryl at the plate. The ball was pitched and Daryl's bat met it with a thundering crack that sent the ball sailing out of sight.

Watching the ball disappear from view, Andy shook his head, gathered up the equipment and ran with the boys towards the house.

"CQ to QC. Come in, QC. Subjects are in sight. Over and out!" Turtle pressed the walkie-talkie close to his mouth but he didn't say anything else. He just stood staring at the driveway. Turtle and Daryl were waiting for Sherie Lee and her date Mark Bennett to come home.

As the motorcycle pulled up, Turtle sprang back to life. "CQ calling QC. Come in, QC. Over."

Daryl was watching TV in his room when he heard Turtle's voice sound over his walkie-talkie.

"This is QC," he answered. "CQ, what's happening? Over."

"QC," Turtle whispered, watching Mark and Sherie Lee hugging, "she's gonna kiss him any second, and right in front of her own home! She's shameless. Oh God, this is disgusting. Over."

Mark gave Sherie a tight squeeze and a tentative peck on the cheek.

"Censored, censored, bleep, bleep, bleep," Turtle called to QC. "Oh, gross, I'm too young to be seeing this."

Turtle leaned out the window to get a better view. Just then, Sherie Lee walked toward the house. Mark followed and ran to hand her something she had left on the bike. Suspiciously, Sherie Lee looked up. Turtle ducked back inside his room. From the street below, his window looked blank for a moment. Then he reappeared and stealthily peered down again.

Daryl sat with the walkie-talkie still in his hands. He was waiting for another update from Turtle on the latest Sherie Lee exploit.

Suddenly Turtle's voice boomed another report. "CQ reporting. His filthy hands are on the butt of her Levi's! He's actually patting her pockets! What a pervert!"

Sherie, overhearing Turtle's commentary, banged on his door and warned him to shut up. Turtle shrugged. "Oh well," he thought, impressed by his own vivid imagination. He was quite satisfied with his invented description of their sexy farewell.

Elaine yelled from her room, "Turtle, will you go to bed already. It's almost midnight!"

Daryl flicked on his "transmit" switch.

"CQ, this is QC. I heard. Good night."

"CQ signing off," Turtle called back. "A little more

educated, a little more shocked by his sister."

Daryl got into bed with his transmitter.

"All knowledge is learning and therefore good. This is QC. Over and out."

.6.

The next morning, Daryl opened the refrigerator door and looked for something to pack for lunch. Dressed in jeans and a sweatshirt, he was almost all ready for school. The radio blared the morning traffic report as he made himself a bologna, mayonnaise and lettuce sandwich. He wrapped the sandwich and threw it into a brown paper bag along with an apple for dessert.

Andy was humming when he entered the kitchen. "Good morning, Daryl. You know, I dreamed about you all night!"

"You did?" Daryl looked surprised.

"You, my friend, are going to *kill* the Warriors!"

Daryl looked startled.

"The big game's on Saturday," Andy reminded him.

"Oh, baseball!" Daryl suddenly realized.

"Sssssshhhh!" Andy winked, holding his finger to his lips. Andy started preparing a pot of coffee.

"Morning, what does everybody want for breakfast today?" Joyce asked as she walked into the kitchen and turned on the faucet.

"I've had mine, thank you," Daryl replied.

"You did?" Joyce finished rinsing her hands.

"I washed the dish."

Joyce looked disappointed. "Oh, okay." She walked over to the refrigerator.

"Now. How about that bologna for your lunchbox?"

Daryl grinned and held up his lunch bag.

"I promised some friends I'd get to school early today and help them..."

"Fine, fine," she said.

Daryl walked over to Joyce, waiting for his good-bye kiss. He looked at her but she merely turned away glumly.

"Are you alright, Joyce?" he asked, putting his hand on her shoulder.

"Sure, fine. I'm just...fine."

She moved close to give Daryl a kiss on the cheek. With his hand still on her shoulder, he pulled her close to him and gave her a big hug. Then he grabbed his lunch and ran out the door.

Joyce felt a little better, but she couldn't fight the fear gnawing at her stomach. She went into Daryl's room and found it just as she expected, tidy, clean, immaculate. She shook her head and looked around a second time. Her stomach grumbled and she left the room, closing the door behind her.

The school bell rang as Daryl, Turtle and few other friends entered the library.

"I can't believe it!" Andrea squealed. "Do it again, Daryl!"

"Ah, it's only a fraud," Hannibal scowled, as Andrea handed Daryl a Rubik's cube. "It's a trick. I saw that magician, what's-his-face, on TV..."

Daryl took the Rubik's cube and turned it around in his hand. It was thoroughly jumbled. With a shy grin, he studied the cube a moment, then, holding it behind his back, he started to twist and turn it.

"It's just a matter of the combination of possible moves and remembering the pattern..." He stopped as the place fell silent.

James Frost, who had been listening to Daryl from behind the library shelves, sauntered across the room.

"Hello," Daryl said, looking directly at Frost.

James ignored Daryl and pushed Turtle roughly against the wall.

"You were laughing at me in class, weren't you, you little pisshead?" Frost said, giving Turtle another rough shove.

"No, I wasn't. I was laughing at a joke. I swear it!"

James laid off Turtle for a moment while he considered his apology.

Turtle perked up and, looking Frost straight in

43

the eyes, laughed, "Yeah, it was just a joke ... a joke called James Frost!" Turtle timed his wisecrack to give him enough time to deliver it and then run to safety. But, his timing was off as Murphy grabbed him and pushed him back towards James.

Turtle tried to fight back, but he was no match for this pair. James pounced on Turtle, punching him with a quick one-two to the jaw and stomach. Another vicious swipe sent Turtle careening into the library shelves, gasping for breath.

Daryl stepped forward, facing James.

"Scum," James sneered at Daryl scornfully. "You seriously think being smart is like being strong?" He pushed Daryl in the chest and sent him stumbling backwards a few paces. Then he grabbed a fistful of Daryl's hair, making him wince in pain. Moving in on Daryl, James hissed, "Turtle had it coming, and now its your turn, scum."

James struck a savage blow to Daryl's eye that sent him reeling. He threw his body on top of Daryl's and delivered blow after blow to his head and face. He lifted Daryl's now limp body up off the floor and gave him another punch in the stomach. With a final kick to the shins, James stepped back to view his work. A winded, bruised Daryl glared at James with pathetic eyes. This time it was James who felt triumphant.

Wanting to have the last word, James warned, "Just remember, I was real easy on you that time ...pal." He turned and started to walk off.

Daryl handed the Rubik's cube to Turtle. It was perfectly arranged. Daryl spoke very softly, "Wait a minute."

James turned back, anticipating another round. He marched up to Daryl and poked him in the chest again. This time Daryl was ready. He moved too fast for James to follow his actions. Grabbing James's wrist, he hoisted himself up behind James's back and flung him to the floor.

Infuriated, James vaulted to his feet and went after Daryl. He started throwing wild punches, but Daryl dodged them like a professional boxer. James tried to kick Daryl, but Daryl caught his foot and twisted his ankle. James's body curled and landed in a heap on the ground.

James was stewing. He quickly righted himself and went after Daryl. But by this time Daryl had him all sized up. He crouched back and tucked his head to his chest. Then with all his might, he clenched his fists, pulled back his arms and rained punches over James's face, chest, and shoulders. James caught the blows and crumpled to the floor. The crowd roared. Finally, James got what he deserved.

That night the Richardsons invited the Foxes over for a barbecue. Howie and Elaine were sprawled out on a couple of lounge chairs, while Joyce flitted about preparing dinner.

Joyce looked at Elaine, "How am I supposed to trust a man like Andy? First he makes Daryl swear to secrecy, then he forces Turtle to take an oath. But it's okay for him to blab the news to me and then shoot off his mouth to you guys."

Andy interrupted. "The only person I don't want to know about this is Bull MacKenzie. He's so cocky that last year he had the nerve to suggest we forfeit the game in the fourth inning."

"Fourth inning?" Howie questioned. "I'm with you, Andy."

"Oh, Andy was brilliant that day," Joyce said sarcastically. "He spiked the Warriors' Cokes with vodka and saved honor. Twenty-two to three, right, champ?"

Elaine gasped. "You're kidding. You know you're lucky you weren't sued. It's against the law to serve alcohol to minors."

Andy grinned. "I didn't serve it."

"So who...?" Elaine stopped short, knowing from the smirk on Andy's face who had played waiter that afternoon. Turtle stood in the doorway with Daryl wondering why Andy was laughing at him.

"We're starving, when's dinner?" he asked.

"You didn't!" Elaine glared at her son.

"Huh?"

"You did. Oh God, Turtle..."

"What'd I do now? I just came in!"

Andy helped Turtle to understand. "Hey Turtle, remember the big game last year? When all the Warriors were thirsty?"

46

"Oh, now I know," Turtle sighed. "Anyway, it wasn't vodka, it was water." Then he winked at Andy and headed out. "Call me when dinner's ready."

Howie yelled after Turtle, "I've got one smart son..."

"You still owe me seven-fifty for the liquor!" Andy added.

Daryl was lingering in the doorway. He asked Andy and Joyce if there was anything he could help them with.

"You could call Sherie Lee," Andy suggested.

"She's gone out," Daryl reported. "With Mark Bennett." He turned to leave.

Elaine sighed at her husband, "What does she see in that boy?"

Daryl turned back to face the adults, stating matter-of-factly, "Sherie Lee says he's sexy. But Turtle says its because he's got the biggest..."

Joyce interrupted, "That's enough, Daryl." Perplexed by Joyce's curt reaction, Daryl walked off in search of Turtle.

Confused, Joyce appealed to Howie, "Tell me, is it me, or..."

"Or what, Joyce?" Howie asked.

"Is there something about Daryl that's a little...?"

Elaine watched Joyce's pained expression. "Howie, let her talk."

"Well, Howie?" Joyce persisted.

Hedging and feeling somewhat trapped, Howie answered Joyce. "He's a nice kid, Joyce. He's just very bright ... I mean bright enough to make you feel that maybe he's, well ... different."

Joyce sighed in resignation, "He's such a good boy. He's so helpful and thoughtful for his age. Maybe that's it ..." She turned to Andy for support. His eyes met hers sympathetically, but he just shrugged. He wasn't going to get himself into this one.

Elaine, feeling uncomfortable with the conversation, argued, "I don't believe what I'm hearing. You're complaining because you got the kind of kid most parents pray for!"

Joyce was taken aback. She hadn't meant to sound so negative. "I'm not complaining," she assured them. "I love Daryl. I mean I really do hope we'll be able to adopt him. It's just that he doesn't seem to ... need anyone."

"Let's eat," Andy called, changing the subject.

The day of the big ballgame had finally come. Dressed in his Little League uniform, Turtle lay on the grass outside his house, eyes closed, calling out to the sky, "Boring, boring, boring. Bo-ring, Borring, B-o-o-ring. *Boring!!!*"

Inside, Daryl and Sherie Lee kept themselves busy playing with her computer. Daryl was fascinated by the versatility of the programs he could run and Sherie Lee was thrilled to have someone so expert share her hobby.

Although Daryl was wearing his Little League uniform, his thoughts were far from the baseball field and the game ahead.

"Did you try the modem?" Sherie Lee asked.

"Is that a game?"

"For someone so smart you sure can be pretty dumb," she smiled, touching the modem.

"This is a modem. It interfaces the computer with other computers through a phone line," she explained. She picked up a magazine and scanned a small ad on the page. "Okay, look. Dial that number on the phone," Sherie Lee instructed as she passed Daryl the magazine.

Daryl dialed the number and Sherie Lee placed the telephone receiver into the modem.

Both of them watched the screen intently, but nothing happened. Sherie fumbled with some keys. "Something's wrong here. We should be getting a list of products..." Suddenly the television screen lit up.

As the computer printed out the information, Elaine passed through the living room and stopped to see what the kids were doing. She glanced at the flickering TV screen, then her eyes focused sharply as she read the list of book titles: LUST FOR LOVE, UNBRIDLED PASSION, DANIELLE'S DESIRES. She stared dumbfounded.

Upstairs in Sherie Lee's room, the computer screen displayed the same book list. "There we go!" exclaimed Sherie Lee. "Computer sales! The hottest new development. You just feed your name and address into the computer and the message is received on the other end. A printer automatically makes out a mailing slip, invoices the purchase request and bills you. Press a few keys and, bingo, you've got yourself a hot new book! You can also use the computer for simple things, like talking to a friend or whatever."

The lesson in computer sales was interrupted by the blaring of a car horn. Daryl could hear Turtle shouting his name.

Daryl touched the modem as Sherie Lee yanked the phone out of its cradle. "I've gotta go play this game," Daryl explained.

"You're not just playing in a *game*," Sherie Lee pointed out. "Bull Mackenzie and your father, uh, Andy, just *hate* each other. Bull's team wins every year. My dad says it's really a pecker contest."

"What's a pecker?"

Sherie Lee groaned and turned away from Daryl. "This is embarrassing!"

The horn continued sounding and it was obvious that Sherie Lee was not going to answer his question, so Daryl bounded down the stairs and ran into the car.

The car was stuffed with baseball gear and at least four other teammates. Daryl jumped into the front seat and was greeted by the gang. Pumped up for the slaughter to come, Andy pressed on the accelerator and tore out.

On the way to the baseball field, Andy stopped at a nearby shopping mall to use the money machine. He left the boys in the car, but waved to Daryl to come join him. Together they walked to the Versatel cash dispenser at the corner of the bank build-ing. As they walked, Andy put an arm around Daryl's shoulder and spoke confidentially.

"I'm going to let you bat fourth, okay? If Jody just bunts and stays put..."

Andy put his card in the slot and punched in his code number. Daryl stood on his tiptoes to read the screen of the money machine. The message read-INSUFFICENT FUNDS.

"Oh, great," Andy groaned. "They screwed up again. There should be fifteen hundred dollars in there..."

Daryl took the card from him. "What's your ID number?" he asked Andy.

"This computer is always screwing up," Andy complained.

"Computers don't make mistakes," Daryl said, "people do. Maybe it was keyed in wrong."

"Twenty-eight twenty-two," Andy replied meekly. He searched his pockets for bills and change to see how much money he had.

Meanwhile, Daryl went to work—fingers flying, machine buzzing. Daryl finished manipulating the computer and turned to Andy, "How much do you want?"

"You got it? Terrific. Let me have a hundred." Daryl pressed some buttons and the machine dis-pensed the money. Andy collected it and asked, "How much does it say I've got there?"

"Oh...enough," Daryl smiled as he looked at the screen with the account of Mr. and Mrs. Andrew G.

Richardson totaling $1,400. A mischievous twinkle brightened Daryl's face. He concentrated hard as he hit a series of computer buttons at incredible speed.

This sequence programmed into the computer simply added a zero to the Richardson balance. Daryl looked at the figure for a moment and then hit one more button. A second zero was added! Andy counted the five twenty-dollar bills and started to walk toward the car. He called over his shoulder, "Come on Daryl, let's go!"

Before following him, Daryl debated whether or not to add one more zero to the balance. What the heck, he figured, and with a little more finger action, the screen was made to read $1,400,000.

As Daryl scampered to join Andy, the mechanical voice of the computer said, "Thank you for banking with United." Daryl turned and smiled, "You're welcome."

.7.

The game was about to begin. The archenemy Warriors and the Mohawks once again took to the field.

Andy and the boys arrived as the Warriors were just finishing up their infield and batting practice. The team was under the militant, gruff instruction of the bull-necked, bug-eyed Bull MacKenzie. The Warriors' uniforms were immaculate, their discipline superb, their sportsmanship the envy of every other team.

What the Mohawks lacked in cleanliness and discipline, they made up for in character. Andy proudly approached Bull MacKenzie. "Well, good luck, Bull," Andy said, offering his hand.

"Luck? Luck didn't win us the championship three years in a row. Teamwork did. Practice. Discipline and teamwork. Luck is for losers, Richardson," MacKenzie shot back.

Andy withdrew his hand but held his steady grin.

Turtle ran up, out of breath. "Arkoff's mother forgot the sodas, so there's none. And there's no ice," he gasped.

Bull MacKenzie looked at Andy with an air of confidence. His snide gaze hinted that this was just the beginning of what was going to be a bad day for Richardson. But Andy could handle this one.

"Now listen, Turtle, run home and tell your mother to bring some soda. But run, Turtle. There's only ten minutes until the game begins!"

Turtle stood rooted to one spot. The command was too much for him. Feeling as if he was going to break under the pressure, he blurted out, "Run? You've got a car!"

Andy stared hard. "Haul ass, Turtle, if you ever want to sit on it again!"

Turtle ran off, his last words barely audible.

Joyce, Elaine and Sherie Lee were standing around the kitchen engaged in some deep conversation.

"Tell me something," Joyce asked, "does Turtle wash his own underwear?"

Elaine muffled a laugh at the very idea. "I don't understand you, Joyce. Daryl's a great kid, why do you always..."

"I know he's a wonderful kid," Joyce interrupted guiltily.

Turtle snuck in through the kitchen door. Before

he was spotted he backed away so he could overhear the rest of the conversation.

"But he's so damned helpful. He doesn't let me help him with anything," Joyce complained.

"He wants to please you," Elaine countered. "Maybe he feels like he owes you something."

"Oh, but Elaine . . . He irons his own clothes, polishes his bedroom floor, gets his own breakfast. He's a better mother than I am!"

Turtle, realizing he only had ten minutes, burst through the doorway panting.

"Sodas. Ice. Mrs. Arkoff forgot. Hurry, the massacre starts in five minutes!"

Frantically, Joyce repeated, "Sodas. Ice." The women moved about the kitchen gathering together the requested items. Elaine mumbled to Joyce, "Keep calm. It'll be all right. You'll see. Now let's go watch our boys play ball."

Turtle, who had overheard his mom's remark, gave the women a curious look as they headed out the door.

By the time Turtle, Joyce, and Elaine got to the ballfield with the soda and ice, the Mohawks were trailing 3–0. Jody barely scratched out a base hit, sending Johnson to second. Daryl took the bat from Andy and paused to receive a quick shoulder rub before leaving the bench. Hannibal and Arkoff sat glumly in the corner of the Mohawk bench. Their morale was steadily slipping.

"It's gonna be another slaughter," Arkoff groaned.

"Maybe we can all fake food poisoning," Hannibal suggested. "I think I could live with that."

Sharing their misery, the boys didn't seem to notice Andy's optimism as he primed Daryl.

"Remember," he coached Daryl, "just meet it."

Daryl walked toward the plate. Joyce and Elaine bent in anticipation as Daryl arrived. A chance to tie was the closest they had ever come. Daryl had no rituals at the plate. He held the bat awkwardly.

"You ever played ball before?" the catcher asked.

"Can it," yelled the umpire.

"Look at him!" the catcher yelled back.

Daryl did look strange. He was loose and unfocused. Until, that is, the first pitch.

His eyes glued on the ball, Daryl swung. The bat connected with a loud, hollow crack. The ball went sailing out of the ballpark! Jody and Johnson watched the ball soar out of the park and turned to see MacKenzie scowling. Daryl stared absentmindedly until Andy's voice jolted him to action.

"Run, Daryl, run!" Daryl ran toward first. Andy shouted after him, "Touch 'em all, Daryl. Touch 'em all!"

The crowd roared wildly. For the first time ever, the Mohawks had tied the Warriors, 3–3.

In the third inning, the Mohawks were trailing again. Daryl was up at bat. Bases were loaded. The pitch was high and outside. Daryl reached out and struck the ball. Again, the ball went sailing out of view. There was an awed silence before the fans cheered loudly. Joyce's eyes followed the ball. Then she turned to see Andy and Daryl jumping up and down, dancing in delight. Somehow she didn't share their excitement; all she felt was an uneasy sense of despair.

Oranges were peeled and the sections were passed out to Mohawk team members. It was between innings, and Daryl was tugging at his mother's shirt-sleeve. He was looking at her cheerfully.

"Andy's so happy," Daryl beamed. "He said we've never been ahead before."

"That's right, Daryl," Joyce said icily. "Not until you came along." She turned away, leaving Daryl surprised by her cool response. He watched as Joyce left the bench without a backward glance. Turtle overheard and gestured to Daryl to join him at the side of the bench.

"Daryl, I've been meaning to give you my speech about grown-ups. It's really a good speech that I meant to give to you weeks ago."

"I've done something to upset her. She's mad at me." Daryl knew that Turtle had seen Joyce walk away.

"No, it's not that's she's mad at you," Turtle said, trying to make his friend feel better. "It's just that grown-ups have to feel like they're making progress with you. You gotta mess up sometimes. I mean, you don't want to mess up so bad that you get whacked, but just enough to make them feel like you're learning something, see? It's a real art."

Daryl looked at Turtle thoughtfully. In the distance there was a shout from the field. The scoreboard changed...Warriors 9, Mohawks 8. Daryl and Turtle were so intent on finishing their talk, they didn't even notice.

"Trust me," Turtle continued. "Leave your room a mess once in a while. Joyce wants to feel useful. You're so damn helpful and good and thoughtful... I don't know why I like you!" Turtle laughed and lightly smacked Daryl on the back.

As the boys talked, the Mohawks struck their third out. The inning was over. The game was at the bottom of the sixth; the score was 9–8.

"Well, that concludes my speech. The lesson being you have to screw up a little. Grown-ups need to get pissed off at their kids every now and then." The two friends exchanged smiles and walked back to the bench.

Joyce returned to the bleachers and grimly resumed watching the game. She couldn't help wondering why Daryl seemed so different from the other boys. She wondered if he would ever need her. Suddenly Elaine dropped back into her seat excitedly.

"Daryl's great, isn't he?" she smiled.

Joyce shot her a pained look and pleaded, "See what I mean?"

Elaine grimaced at the mistake. The game continued and Jody finally got the hit he was waiting for. Running like a bat out of hell, he rounded first base and headed for second. A bad throw by the Warriors gave Jody the chance to go for the long-dreamed-of home run. Ducking and weaving, he slid into home plate and was called...safe! This surely had to be the best moment of his life!

Daryl approached the plate. It was his turn up at bat. The team looked his way expectantly. The first ball was pitched.

"Strike one!" yelled the umpire.

Andy stared, horrified. "Strike," he thought. "On Daryl?"

The pitch, a swing and the loud bellowing of the umpire calling, "Strike two!"

Daryl turned and scowled at him. "Strike?" he called back. "Why don't you open your eyes?"

With that remark, the umpire exploded in anger. "One more crack out of you and you're history! Got it?"

Daryl ignored the threat and just looked back at the pitcher. The pitcher wound up and let loose the ball. Daryl swung and was called out. "Strike three, you're out!"

Turtle closed his eyes in despair. He didn't mean for Daryl to start messing up now. As Daryl walked off the field, Turtle ran toward him, muttering beneath his breath. "Listen, there's no need to blow the whole game, I mean..."

Daryl shot him a serious look. "You think the

game's more important than Joyce?" He strode toward the bench.

Three strikes, Joyce thought, feeling suddenly relieved. He's struck out. Her boy was fallible after all. Perhaps he could use a bit of motherly consoling.

Daryl dropped the bat as he returned to the bench. "What happened?" Andy asked. Daryl shrugged and didn't reply. Joyce walked up as Andy was pressing Daryl for an answer.

"Daryl, what went wrong?" he asked again, seeing Joyce approach.

"I don't even like the game," Daryl shouted, suddenly getting red in the face. "I mean, all it is is a pecker contest between you and MacKenzie!"

"What?" Andy and Joyce gasped.

"Daryl!" Joyce said in her most motherly, stern voice. "That's no way to talk to Andy!"

"Kiss my ass!" he shouted, as he turned his back to them and walked away from the bench. Andy stood there shocked beyond belief. He would have never thought Daryl was capable of behaving in such a rude manner. "I don't believe it . . . ," he said shaking his head. Then, turning after the boy, he called, "Daryl, wait! Come back!"

Joyce was hurt that Daryl would talk that way to Andy. She felt both angry and glad. Daryl had no right to be disrespectful, but it was a refreshing change. As she neared Andy and Turtle, she could hear Andy saying, "Well, there goes the game."

"We could make a deal with him," Turtle suggested. "He'll hit another one . . . if you kiss his ass."

The teammates watching the incident started to laugh, then were quieted by Joyce's parting remark.

"Andy wants to win so bad, he'd probably do it."

Joyce found Daryl outside of the ballpark. He was pushing around some dirt with his foot. Joyce knelt behind him and gently touched his shoulder. Daryl slowly turned around and faced Joyce. "Daryl, honey . . . there's something we should talk about . . ." Joyce hedged.

"I guess I really screwed up, didn't I?"

"It's all right to . . . to screw up sometimes . . . Everybody does."

"Yeah, well, that's what Turtle, I mean, that's what I figured. But," he asked anxiously, "is it really all right?"

"Of course it is, only . . . " she hesitated, trying to figure out how to say it. "Well, your language . . . "

Remembering what he'd said, Daryl looked into her eyes. "Not too good, huh?"

Joyce shook her head. "Mm-hm."

"I'd like to apologize for that, Joyce. Next time I screw up, I'll watch my mouth."

Daryl felt confused and unhappy at his behavior. Sensing Daryl's sadness, Joyce grabbed him and hugged him lovingly. He hugged her back and they both smiled. Then he turned and walked away. Joyce gazed after Daryl, wondering about this solemn, curious child.

Daryl returned to the ballfield. It was the bottom of the seventh. The Mohawks were trailing by two runs. Hannibal was on second. Arkoff on third. Turtle picked up the bat and walked to the plate. He mustered and cut at the first pitch. Foul tip. Strike one.

Daryl watched from the fence, anxious for the next ball. The pitch was thrown. Turtle's bat connected, sending a solid line drive out across the field. The crowd howled with delight as Turtle took off. Arkoff ran. Hannibal ran. Bull MacKenzie, red as a beet, screamed at his outfielders.

The crowd gasped as they followed the ball. The left fielder lunged, but the ball just eluded his outstretched mitt and careened off the fence. Arkoff was home! Hannibal was thundering toward home! Turtle swerved toward third. The left fielder retrieved the ball and pegged it home. Andy ran along the baseline, shouting, "Hit the dirt, Turtle!" Turtle slid headfirst across the plate under the catcher's tag.

Howls rang out from the team and the bleachers full of onlookers. "Three runs! They won!"

Daryl leaped in the air, yelping with delight. Turtle threw his cap on the ground and looked around as if he'd heard Daryl's shout of joy.

The win was too much for Andy, who went berserk, hugging the players, slapping them on the back, all the while looking around for Daryl. Even big-necked Bull MacKenzie forced himself to remember the code of the sportsman, and with a plastic grin of congratulations on his face, he shook Andy's hand. Andy called the team together for a victory cheer as a local photographer snapped a picture of the victorious Mohawks for the evening edition of the newspaper.

.8.

The Pentagon's information-gathering system operated around the clock on a complex machinery system, scanning newspapers and information sources around the globe. The machines hummed softly, silently digesting and sorting the information, keyed to highlighted areas, that was deemed to be matters of national security. Specific words were singled out: *Soviet; security; infiltration.* The machines scanned every sentence written and selected relevant passages, which were automatically photocopied.

Moments after the photocopy was made, a message was superscripted on a selected newspaper item. REFER SECTION D2...FURTHER INQUIRY, ARLINGTON...REFER O'SEAS BUREAU...REFER SECTION D2...PRIORITY TO PENTAGON DEPARTMENT Y...

The Barkenton Weekly was fed into the machine for scanning. On the front page was a photograph of Turtle and Daryl under the headline WARRIORS WALLOPED BY MOHAWK STARS. The machine isolated Turtle for a moment and then moved on the Daryl. It responded by examining his photograph more closely. Closer still. Then it ripped at eye-bending speed through a file of photographs of other children before stopping on a file photograph of Daryl. The machine worked without undue emphasis, merely recording another item.

The superscript read: REFER TASCOM URGENT ... TASCOM PRIORITY.

Joyce attempted to show Daryl how to read music. "Now," she explained patiently, "between the lines, the notes are F, A, C, E, but only in the treble clef."

"Okay," Daryl said, nodding in agreement. "And those are E, G, B, D and F with the right hand. *Every good boy does fine*," he added with a smile.

"You got it," Joyce cheered.

Pointing at the page, Daryl repeated, "Whole beat, two half-beats, four quarters to a beat." With his right hand he picked out a simple melody from the music.

Andy and his crew had just finished their review of some building plans when Howie approached.

"Howie ... Great you stopped by. You want to help

yourself to coffee ... ? I'll be right back."

"Andy, it's taking all I got just coming here..."

Andy saw the gravity and agony on his friend's face. "What is it?" he asked, walking quickly to Howie's side.

"I've been contacted by lawyers acting on behalf of Daryl's parents." Howie blurted out the words unevenly.

"His parents ...?"

"They've been tracing him for months," Howie explained. "I'm afraid there's no doubt, Andy. He's their son."

Andy closed his eyes against the painful reality. Daryl was someone else's son.

.9.

The news of Daryl's real parents' existence hit Joyce hard. She sat pale and gaunt in Howie's office at the Barkenton Child Care Facility. Andy, too, was drained of all emotion. The pair stared into space as they waited for Elaine to look up from the mass of papers on her desk.

"If there was anything I could do," Elaine said helplessly, "anything, you know I'd find a way to do it."

Andy suddenly jerked in his seat and focused on Elaine. "How can we even know he's theirs?"

"Andy, there's no doubt he's their child. Look, even the photographs..."

She pointed to two or three photographs of Daryl on the edge of her desk. The pictures showed him at different ages, but all of them posed him against the same flat, gray backdrop. The photos were strangely anonymous and devoid of feeling.

Joyce picked one up to look at it for the hundredth time. "What kind of people are they?" she cried. "I mean...didn't they ever take him to the beach?"

She dropped the photograph back on the desk as a sob escaped her throat and she covered her eyes. Andy tightened his arm around her and tried to comfort her, though he knew it was hopeless.

Standing in his bedroom, Daryl stared out the window, lost in thought. Andy peeked in and entered hesitantly, fearing what he had to say and not wanting to have to say it.

"Daryl?" Andy called softly as the boy he had come to think of as his son turned to him. "How're you doing?"

"I'm all right, thanks," he said solemnly.

"Listen," Andy began, "...can we talk a while?"

"Of course." Daryl walked over to Andy politely, serious and grave, ready to listen.

Andy cleared his throat, his eyes filling with tears. "I, uh...I just thought we might...I mean, uh...I mean, maybe we should..." He shuffled awkwardly, searching for the words.

"Why don't you sit down?" Daryl suggested.

"Yeah, thanks," Andy said, gratefully sitting on the boy's bed. He nearly stopped short, realizing that Daryl was making the effort to put him at ease, rather than vice versa, which was what he had intended. "I just want you to know ... Well, I guess you already know how much Joyce and I are going to miss you ..."

"I know. Me too," Daryl said sincerely.

"Yeah." Andy dropped his eyes to the floor before he could go on. "Well, anyhow ... The point is you're going back home, and that's something that should make you happy."

"I'm trying, Andy, but," he stopped, looking oddly confused, "... it doesn't *mean* anything!"

"That'll change, Daryl, you'll see, as soon as you're back where you ... your home."

Daryl gazed sadly at Andy. "I feel like *this* is my home."

Hearing this, Andy turned briefly, tears trickling down his face. He wiped his eyes and put his arm around Daryl.

"Daryl, your parents love you and they're your real parents and they've been looking for you for months. They want you back, and that's ..."

"But what if I want to be with you?" Daryl interrupted.

"Children belong to their parents," Andy said flatly.

"Like your car belongs to you?" the boy asked.

"No, oh God, no, not like that," Andy cried, as he struggled to convince himself of this truth. "Look ... I'm sure that when you get back home your

71

memory'll start to come back...You'll remember all kinds of good times, and friends...you'll see, it'll be fine."

"Dad...I mean, Andy," Daryl said, looking up.

"Yeah...?"

"I won't forget *you*, will I?"

"Of course you won't. We'll keep in touch."

Andy hugged the boy close to him as he looked out the window. He didn't feel very convinced of this himself.

Joyce came into the room and the trio stood silently together, sadly aware that it might be for the last time. Andy and Daryl sat on the bed, while Joyce peered out the window, slowly pulling back the curtain as she spotted the late-model blue sedan slowing down in front of the house.

That must be Daryl's mother, Joyce thought to herself, vaguely uncomfortable as she watched the crisply efficient woman in her late thirties who was sitting in the driver's seat. She focused next on the man, considerably older than the woman, who sat in the passenger seat.

Joyce turned to face Daryl. "They look really nice," she said, putting on a brave face. She busied herself by straightening the neck of Daryl's pullover and checking his general appearance.

"Okay. I guess that's as good as you're going to look," she said, half smiling. "You okay?"

Daryl nodded his head solemnly, not sure what was expected of him in the next hour.

"So, how about getting ready to give your mom and dad a big smile, huh?"

The trio walked arm in arm from the room. Daryl turned and took a long look back, sighing as he closed the door.

Outside, Ellen Lamb and Dr. Jeffrey Stewart got out of the car in front of the Richardson house and headed up the walk.

Andy answered the ring at the door.

"Mr. Richardson? I'm Jeffrey Stewart. This is my wife, Ellen."

"I'm pleased to meet you," Andy said. "Please come in." He watched the couple curiously as they entered. The man seemed alert and intelligent, but softer and kinder than his wife, who was altogether cooler and more detached.

Closing the door behind them, Andy led them into the living room.

Dr. Stewart paced nervously.

"Probably anxious to see your son again?" Andy offered.

"Is Daryl ... I mean he's ... quite all right?" Stewart asked.

"He's a tremendous young man," Andy said enthusiastically. "We certainly, uh, envy you your son. He'll be right down. Probably just a little ... nervous ... you know how kids get?"

Stewart looked up, surprised. "Daryl—nervous?"

Dismissing the thought with a wave of his hand, Andy said, "Can I offer you a drink or something?"

Stewart shook his head. "Mr. Richardson, I want you to know how much I, I mean, my wife and I appreciate the kindness you've shown Daryl."

"It wasn't hard. He's a great kid," Andy said with a sad smile.

Looking at Andy with an odd, piercing gaze, Stewart observed, "You've formed a considerable attachment to him, I can see."

"That's an understatement," Andy said with a strained laugh. "We're going to miss him. Both of us. A lot."

Stewart had been staring at Andy with his curiously penetrating eyes. He suddenly nodded his head, as though Andy's attachment to Daryl gave him some profound inner satisfaction.

"Yes," he said, seeming to regain his composure. "Of course you will, of course."

Andy looked from the man to the woman as Stewart seemed to dart a look of triumph her way. The exchange puzzled Andy and troubled Ellen Lamb.

The sound of footsteps on the staircase broke the momentary awkwardness as Daryl and Joyce entered the room. Daryl gazed at his parents with rapt attention but did not say a word.

Dr. Stewart stepped forward formally and crouched to gaze searchingly into the boy's eyes. "Daryl . . . ? Do you remember us?"

Daryl looked from one to the other, trying to recall. Stewart remained crouched before him. His mother stood aloof but smiling with a kind of expectancy.

"I think...I do."

Ellen walked to his side, but did not touch him. Her voice was kind, but impersonal, like that of a nurse or nanny, not like that of a mother who had not seen her son for many months.

Joyce barely breathed as she watched the exchange.

"You're just fine, Daryl," Ellen said mechanically. "There's nothing to worry about. Do you want to go and get your things?"

Daryl's head suddenly jerked back to look at Joyce, who was biting her lip hard.

"Isn't Turtle coming over?" Daryl almost cried. "I can say good-bye to Turtle, can't I?"

Down the street, Turtle was as upset at the thought of Daryl leaving as Joyce and Andy were.

Chin quivering, he listened as his mother urged him not to avoid the painful good-bye.

"Turtle, it's normal to feel bad about losing a friend. But you can't just duck out and not say good-bye. Daryl's expecting you to be there. He'll need you to be th—"

"But Mom...!" Turtle wailed.

"You promised him. Now I want you to come with me right now—and show your best friend you haven't forgotten about him already."

Turtle hung his head, ashamed, as a tear trickled down his cheek.

"Let's go," Elaine ordered as they marched out the door.

"Daryl, why don't you get your things?" his mother instructed as the adults attempted to make conversation. He went upstairs and gazed out the window of his bedroom, waiting for a sign of his friend. His last few remaining things were packed in a grip bag on the bed. He looked out again toward Turtle's house. Suddenly he saw Elaine and Turtle heading his way. Daryl started running down the stairs to meet him.

Tears swelled in Turtle's eyes and he wiped his nose on the sleeve of his shirt. Up ahead he saw Darly run out from the Richardson house, waiting for him. Turtle stopped in his tracks. "I can't go through with it!" Turtle cried as he turned and ran down the street.

Elaine turned around. He was gone.

"Turtle...!" she called after him.

Daryl watched Turtle's escape in disbelief. He stared after his friend, confused and hurt by his disappearance.

"Daryl...?" Stewart's voice made Daryl turn around.

"I saw what happened with your friend," he said kindly. "Do you understand why he did that?"

Daryl shook his head. "Is he mad at me?"

"I don't think so. I think he's going to miss you,

and that makes it hard to say good-bye."

Daryl turned back to look where Turtle had run, thinking about what Stewart had said. Elaine waved apologetically.

"Can you imagine how he must feel?" Stewart continued.

Shaking his head slowly, Daryl admitted, "Yes, I can."

"That's good, Daryl," Stewart answered with a quiet pride. "That's very good."

Stewart put his arm on Daryl's shoulder and led the boy to the waiting car.

Turtle hid behind a building around the corner from the Richardson house, sobbing. He looked up as he heard the car's engine start and peered through a narrow gap between the buildings.

"I can't believe it, he's really going." Turtle sobbed as he watched the car drive away. He sat leaning against the building with his head in his hands.

"It's okay," his mother consoled, as she reached gently for his shoulder and cradled him in her arms. "You're forgiven."

"Good-bye," Daryl waved solemnly from the back seat.

Joyce turned away, tears blinding her eyes, as Andy stepped forward and put his hand on the glass. Daryl's hand met Andy's from the other side of the window. As they waved, the car carried Daryl into the distance and out of sight.

.10.

Speeding away from Barkenton and the place he'd called home, Daryl sat alone in the back of the plush car, saddened, yet excited at the prospect of an adventure ahead. Ellen Lamb and Dr. Stewart sat rigid and silent in the front seat. The trio traveled for less than an hour when the car pulled into what seemed to be an unmarked military airbase.

"Are we going to fly?" Daryl asked, his curiosity mounting as he saw an unmarked Grumman jet waiting on the field. "We're going to fly in that?" His enthusiasm rose.

A pilot in civilian clothes stepped out of the plane as the car approached and stood at attention waiting for it to stop. As the pilot opened the door, Daryl jumped from the car and ran around the plane, looking at it from every angle.

"Well, Ellen, what do you think?" Stewart asked, watching Daryl.

"Frankly, Doctor, I think it's remarkable," she replied coolly.

As Daryl tasted the first hours of this new life, his old "family" tried to come to terms with their loss.

"You know something I don't understand?" Andy asked Joyce, Elaine and Howie as they sat around the kitchen table. "They just didn't ask anything. You know? I mean about Daryl."

"Like those pictures they showed us," Joyce added as she turned to Howie. "So anonymous. Daryl just ...standing against some wall."

"It seemed like all they wanted was to get him out of here before anyone asked anything," Andy mused.

"What d'you think?" he asked Howie. Howie shook his head, "Look, I know how you feel..."

"It's a terrible shock," Elaine interrupted, "but you were prepared for it, you knew it might happen."

"We'll find you another child," Howie promised. "Before you know it, you'll..."

"*No!*" Joyce cried out. "Not another child. I want Daryl."

Dr. Stewart lit a cigarette as Daryl turned to him.

"Can I go see the pilot now?" Daryl asked, thrilled to be flying.

"Sure," he smiled. "Ask him anything you want!"

Daryl walked toward the cockpit and opened the small door. Inside, the pilot and copilot sat side by side. The pilot turned and smiled as Daryl entered.

"Hi there, Daryl, come on in. So you want to learn to fly this thing, huh?"

Examining the instrument panel intently, Daryl answered, "I'd find it very interesting."

"Okeedoke," the pilot said. "Here you've got altitude, airspeed and engine thrust." He pointed to the various instruments and buttons and continued the explanation. "This is your horizon level indicator. These are flip and elevator controls which along with the stick are the basic guidance mechanisms..." Daryl followed with rapt attention.

Back in the cabin, Stewart celebrated a quiet victory, sipping a drink.

"You know, the extraordinary thing is that we've accomplished something by accident that we could never have dared by intent—putting him out there just to see what happened," Stewart said to Ellen. "When Dr. Mulligan 'kidnapped' him, he did the best work of his career."

"You were right about its learning potential," Ellen agreed.

"No, I was wrong," Stewart said. Ellen looked puzzled. "I suspect he's learned more than I thought possible."

"Even with the amnesia factor," she said coldly.

"He's a very special little boy," Stewart mused, looking toward the cockpit in front of him.

□ □ □

"As backup to the computer you should check visually. Okay, here's the navigation chart we're on now...," the pilot continued.

"We're there, right?" Daryl asked, pointing to the chart.

"Hey, you've really been listening!" the copilot laughed. "You take that figure from the trip computer, insert your coordinates, airspeed, wind factor and time calculations. Then you ask the computer to calculate...," he explained, as his fingers flew over the keyboard and dials.

"And the figures ought to match your own rough calculation of...28394," he said.

"Six," Daryl corrected, as the computer printout emerged.

The copilot looked up at Daryl, not understanding. "What?"

Suddenly embarrassed, Daryl said meekly, "28396. You said four. But on the data base given it's 28396."

The copilot hurriedly ripped off the printout to check this figure. "Well, I'll be...," he stammered.

"Kid's after your job, Major, uh, Harry," the pilot beside him laughed.

Staring fixedly at the control panels, Daryl muttered, "So if I wanted to go back home I'd just... feed in the coordinates and instruct the auto pilot..."

The pilot looked at Daryl, shook his head and continued, "That's right, program them in and send to the auto control center, right..."

Daryl's hands remained at his sides. He did not touch any of the dials or switches. But quite suddenly, the plane banked steeply, turning 180 degrees with a sudden surge of power, pointing back in the direction of Barkenton.

The pilot and copilot were stunned. They responded with practiced efficiency.

"Manual control."

"Manual control, check," the copilot confirmed. He hit four switches. The pilot took control and eased the aircraft back onto its flight path. They looked at each other, confused by the sudden maneuver, and unable to explain the sudden change in direction.

"You better go back to your parents before we hit any more of these . . . air pockets," the pilot said to Daryl.

Daryl smiled politely. "Thank you for showing me everything."

The copilot ushered him out, fast. When the door was closed, he turned back to his colleague, ashen-faced. "What the hell was that?" he asked.

Daryl slipped back into the cabin silently, sadly. Dr. Stewart and Ellen Lamb did not notice his reentry. He stood quietly, listening to a snatch of their conversation, as Ellen firmly pressed her point to Stewart.

"Doctor, whatever we do, there's no way it can ever be classified as 'normal.' I thought that was understood when we . . ."

A signal from Stewart silenced her. He saw Daryl listening. There was sudden alarm on the boy's face.

"Well now, Daryl? Did you see everything up front?"

"Yes, thank you."

"Why don't you come sit down and let Ell...your mom fix you some juice or something."

Daryl slumped into his seat glumly.

"What'll you have Daryl?" Ellen looked at the boy and saw him stare down at the floor. He straightened up suddenly and looked directly at the two strangers.

"Are you really my mom and dad?" he asked. Daryl registered the quick look of uneasiness that passed between the adults before they could hide it. Ellen bent on one knee by his seat. Her grave face betrayed the reassurance she tried to put into words.

"Yes, Daryl," she replied. "We are."

Daryl wrinkled his brow and turned from the woman, peering out at the clouds beyond. He did not answer.

.11.

The TASCOM building, a division of the Pentagon, stood vast and forbidding, a concrete and black glass structure standing like a mirage in the midst of nondescript emptiness. Cars were parked on leveled wasteland. There was no sign of human life.

Inside the furturistic building, a spherical space resembling a huge operating room was brilliantly lit from translucent walls which were split by two long observation windows. In the center of the space, spread-eagled on a slab of gleaming steel, Daryl was strapped like a specimen under glass in a natural history museum. Binding restrained his torso, wrists and ankles. He lay unconscious. A motorized arc moved above him, halting at a 45-degree horizontal angle.

Dressed in a white lab coat, Dr. Stewart stood before a bank of monitoring equipment, surrounded by several assistants. As he touched a control, a strange inverted-U-shaped arm slid silently out of the wall of the spherical chamber and traveled along, inches above Daryl's body. Ellen Lamb stood behind Stewart, her eyes riveted on the small and helpless figure of the child.

Dr. Stewart turned to watch a television monitor to his right. A high definition image of Daryl's scan appeared, transparent as an X-ray. The "scanner" continued moving up Daryl's body past his beating heart and onto his skull. But instead of the outline of an organic brain, the monitor focused on a much more symmetrical pattern of labyrinthine circuitry and microchip technology. Daryl's brain was a computer!

Adjusting a control, Stewart looked closer at the image.

"The problem's somewhere," he paused, turning several more controls, "here."

"Let's get a close-up of that small area of the electronic brain," Stewart ordered, focusing on a mass of infinitely finer detail. Stewart punched another switch and lines shot out from various circuits with identifying code numbers at the ends.

"There it is," Stewart said, pointing to the one code number flashing red and white which stood out from the rest.

"Can you reactivate the memory without surgery?" Ellen asked.

"My guess is that Dr. Mulligan only provoked specific overload, not a burnout," Stewart said. "I think at some stage he'd have wanted Daryl to know what he was. We'll soon see."

Stewart punched more switches. The TV screen focused on even more detailed pictures. Daryl's face twitched and his eyes moved under their lids but did not open. A powerful buzz of electric current filled the chamber. Stewart looked up from the screen and out to Daryl's prone body. "Okay, let's try talking to him," he said.

Swinging his chair to another computer keyboard, he punched up a question, which was displayed on the screen above it: WHAT IS YOUR NAME?

Daryl's eyes continued to twitch beneath their lids. A reply appeared on the screen: DARYL.

Stewart waited a moment, then punched in another instruction: REPLY INCOMPLETE. PLEASE EXPAND

A pause followed. Suddenly, the letters on the screen shuffled apart and a period was added after each one: D.A.R.Y.L.

Stewart looked up at Ellen Lamb with relief and pleasure on his face. He checked further, punching in: PLEASE EXPLAIN ACRONYM. The screen lit up: DATA-ANALYZING ROBOT YOUTH LIFE-FORM. Stewart turned to Ellen beaming with triumph. He punched a last message into the keyboard: WELCOME BACK, DARYL. A moment later a reply appeared: THANK YOU, SIR. The initial test completed, Daryl was moved from the operating chamber.

□ □ □

Day ran into night in the adjacent computer room, where banks of machines with winking lights and slowly turning spools of tape worked constantly. The acronym D.A.R.Y.L. was emblazoned above the whole installation. Ellen stood looking over yards of printout rattling into a tray. Stewart ambled up to her. Reading over her shoulder, he said, "Frankly, I'm beginning to understand why Dr. Mulligan did what he did."

Steadily studying the printout, Ellen did not raise her eyes, but answered, "He was supposed to be a scientist."

"I'm puzzled, Ellen, by your determination to see Daryl as nothing more than a machine."

"That's what it is, Doctor. A machine."

"Dr. Mulligan thought we'd created something more. That's why he thought we should stop the research."

"Is that what you think, Doctor?" Ellen asked, raising her eyes.

"No," Stewart said, "but this is a breakthrough. Daryl has picked up more than he was programmed to learn."

"That's a matter of opinion," Ellen countered.

"I accept the challenge," Stewart said. "Let's see."

Stewart and Ellen moved into a video screening room where they called up the computer memory of Daryl's first computer video game, Pole Position.

"It's amazing," Ellen admitted, watching Daryl's

hands on the controls of the game.

"Let's see if we can get some input from Daryl on the learning process," Stewart suggested. He pressed a button, and Daryl, awake and alert, was sent into the screening room. Daryl sat between Stewart and Ellen as they all looked at a picture, frozen on the enlarged screen, of the boy playing the video game.

Stewart turned to the boy. "Daryl, what did you feel about being so good at that game?"

Reflecting a moment, Daryl said, "I didn't feel anything. I just...did it."

"Okay," Stewart said, pressing another switch, "the ballgame."

The screen changed and Daryl was up at bat at the big Mohawks–Warriors baseball game. He swung and hit the ball out of the park.

"What made you change the way you were playing after Turtle spoke to you that day?" Stewart asked.

Daryl paused and thought before answering. "I interpreted this data to indicate that under certain conditions, error was more efficient than maximum performance."

"Under what conditions?" Stewart pressed.

"Relating with others," Daryl replied as Stewart and Ellen exchanged a brief glance.

"Okay," Stewart challenged Ellen, "what do you say to that?"

"Perception of the optimum. The program was designed for it," she shot back.

Stewart punched up a third series of images for review.

"Come on, man, make up your mind," Turtle whined to Daryl on the screen. "D'you want chocolate or vanilla?" Turtle waved two bowls of ice cream in Daryl's direction. He was surrounded by about a dozen kids in Turtle's house, including Trudi, Andrea, Hannibal, Jody and Arkoff. They were seated around a table, stuffing their faces with sandwiches, jello and ice cream.

Daryl looked at Turtle and the ice cream with uncertainty. "I don't know, I..."

"Well, try some," Turtle said, handing Daryl a spoon with a small scoop of chocolate. Daryl tasted the ice cream. "Hmmm...yeah, well...," Daryl said, savoring the taste.

"Shit, Daryl, if you don't care, take the vanilla," Turtle yelled impatiently, plonking a bowl of vanilla ice cream in front of his friend. Daryl handed the chocolate over to some other kid. He dipped his spoon in for a taste of the vanilla. After a moment he said, "Turtle, I like the chocolate better."

Turtle turned to him with long-suffering patience. "Can I assume this is a final decision?"

"Absolutely."

"Okay."

Turtle reached rudely across the table and snatched the chocolate ice cream back from the girl he had given it to.

"Mary Ellen, wait!" Turtle yelled. "Don't eat that! Daryl just spit into it!"

"That's disgusting," Mary Ellen cried, wrinkling her nose. She pulled away from the bowl of chocolate ice cream as though it were poison. Sherie Lee glared at Turtle, who banged the bowl down in front of Daryl.

Stewart stopped the picture. He watched Daryl closely.

"Did you really mean it—that you preferred chocolate?" he asked.

"Oh, sure."

"Why?"

A blank look came over Daryl's face. "I . . . I don't know . . . I just did," he said, shrugging. "Turtle likes raspberry."

"But there's no difference," Stewart told him.

A look of amusement crossed Daryl's face. He looked at the Doctor as if he just didn't understand kids.

"They *taste* different," he explained.

Stewart looked over to Ellen. "He's not ever *programmed* for taste."

"It's programmed to *learn*," Ellen insisted.

"Not subjective preferences," Stewart countered. "He can analyze nutritional values, not choose between flavors."

"So it's picking up behavior patterns," Ellen admitted.

"Please stop calling him 'it'!" Stewart insisted.

Daryl turned to the man. "Thank you," he said sincerely.

The two scientists looked at each other in silence

until Stewart concluded, "We'll have to run physical tests. Trial and error till we find where this comes from."

.12.

Bright fluorescent lights shined down on Daryl's frightened face as the small robot-boy was strapped to an operating table. Bustling about him were white-coated scientists and assistants, including Stewart and Ellen. Steel bands and electrodes were fixed to Daryl's head. Banks of monitoring equipment surrounded him. He was awake and alert, his opened eyes darting nervously around the cold hospital setting.

Seeing the fear in the boy's eyes, Dr. Stewart walked to his side, next to the operating table. "Daryl, don't worry," Stewart reassured him. "You know you can't come to any harm. You know that."

Daryl did not respond.

Gently, Stewart asked, "Are you feeling...scared?

You were never designed to feel that way. I'm sorry if you are. But I promise we won't hurt you."

Daryl looked up at the doctor. "Why do you have to do this? What are you going to do?"

"We're just going to take some samples. You won't feel it. But we do need you to be conscious."

Daryl turned his head slightly, just as a nurse approached wheeling a tray of sharp surgical instruments. As Daryl spotted the tray, an anxious cry came from across the room.

"Dr. Stewart!" An assistant stood at a monitoring machine whose dials and graphs were going crazy.

"What's going on ...?" Stewart asked the assistant.

"It just started, sir."

Suddenly another yell came from another corner of the room.

"Doctor!" another assistant called, pointing to a second machine which had just gone berserk.

"This is crazy!" A third assistant said, running from machine to machine. "It's like someone is playing around with the central computer."

Stewart turned and looked, as bedlam took over the quiet of the sterile operating room. Suddenly his eye caught a message flickering on a computer screen.

I'M FRIGHTENED! it read.

The scientist stopped, shocked. Then he looked over at Daryl and crossed to the boy's side again. He looked down into the anxious face with a curious mixture of concern and suspicion.

Gently he put his hand on the boy's shoulder. "All right, Daryl," Stewart said quietly, "...forget the tests. No tests. All right?"

Daryl looked up. He closed his eyes in relief. A half smile crossed his lips and he relaxed at once.

A new message appeared on the screen: THANK YOU.

General Lyford Graycliffe sat at his desk in the Pentagon reading through a page or two of notes. He was a lean man with clear blue eyes, extremely young to be a general.

Three other military personnel, two in civilian clothing, and all of lower rank, sat nearby. The four clearly comprised a committee, with Graycliffe as chairman. Dr. Stewart sat at a desk opposite the general, addressing the committee.

"On top of the learning factor, he seems to have developed an ability to interface directly with computers," Stewart said, detailing developments in the D.A.R.Y.L. project.

"How does that work?" the general asked, flipping a page.

"I'm not sure yet," Stewart admitted. "It's most likely some kind of magnetic field. He isn't even conscious of his power..."

The general looked up from his papers, suddenly realizing the significance of what Stewart was saying. "Your report makes some pretty extraordinary claims, Doctor Stewart."

"Simple observations, General," Stewart replied.

"You're now saying it can...feel human emotion?" one of the other men asked.

"He experiences pleasure and pain, he also registers anxiety and fear," said Stewart.

A slight smile played on the general's lips. "Fear is something we don't have a lot of use for on this project."

"We?" Stewart asked suspiciously.

"The people who are funding your research, doctor," the general replied.

"The American tax payer?" asked Stewart.

The general ignored Stewart's sarcasm. "When your colleague, Dr. Mulligan, ran off with this expensive piece of hardware, I didn't hear you bleating on behalf of the tax payer."

"Because thanks to Mulligan's mistakes, we now know far more about Daryl's potential than we did before."

"Baseball, ice cream and friendships are all right for America," Graycliffe said. "But hardly what we need at the Department of Defense. The joint chiefs have made their decision in the light of this report. The youth lifeform project, as of now, is terminated."

Stewart slumped in his chair, defeated.

One of the military men spoke. "The department has set out its requirements in this work paper. Basically, we need an adult version of this prototype. Programmed to learn and then taught everything the army can teach a fearless, technically skilled, devastating *soldier*..."

The general looked squarely at the doctor with hard-set eyes. "D.A.R.Y.L. goes to the scrap yard. Understood, Doctor?" he commanded.

Stewart dropped his head at the command.

.13.

"Hi, Daryl. What's up?" Dr. Stewart called loudly over the din of the noisy room. He covered his ears with his hands as he walked into Daryl's igloo-shaped windowless dome at TASCOM headquarters. Daryl sat watching six TV sets, each one blaring away. The noise was deafening.

"Shall I turn them off?" Daryl asked innocently as Stewart pointed toward the sets.

"Maybe down a little," the doctor smiled. He looked around at the books, computer games, high-tech toys and functional furniture which filled the room.

Daryl didn't move. He glanced toward a small computer tuner with a brief show of concentration. Suddenly the room was silent.

"They want to know how you do that," Stewart said, looking at Daryl. "Matter of fact, so do I."

"I'm not sure. I can kind of 'read' what a computer's doing."

"And control it?" Stewart asked.

"I guess." Daryl shrugged. "I'm getting better at it."

"But people," Stewart asked, "you can't tell what they're thinking, can you?"

"Oh no, I'm not telepathic or anything."

"Then how do you know what they're *feeling?*"

"Well, you sort of guess at that—because you know what you're feeling yourself," the boy explained.

Stewart reflected on the statement a moment.

Daryl broke the silence. "I wondered if...maybe ...you'd let Andy and Joyce visit me," he asked, a tremble of excitement in his voice. "I would...very much...like to see them."

"How could I not grant what may be Daryl's last wish?" Stewart thought to himself in agony.

"And your friend, what's his...?"

"Turtle!" Daryl beamed. "I'd like that! I miss them, I really do."

Stewart looked at the boy with a smile of understanding on his face. "All right, then we'll tell them the truth," he said, standing up and looking affectionately at Daryl from across the room.

Daryl smiled back at the doctor. "Dr. Stewart,... what am I?" he asked, bewildered and concerned.

Not answering, the doctor turned to leave as emotion choked his voice.

Through an observation window to Daryl's room, Ellen Lamb watched the exchange between Stewart and the boy.

She did not turn around when Stewart entered the room.

"What *is* he, Ellen?"

Ellen Lamb ignored the philosophical question and quickly changed the subject. "You're not really going to bring those people here, are you?" she asked incredulously.

"I can give security clearance to anyone I choose. Unless the military override me, and there's no reason why they should," he said, looking pointedly at his colleague, "is there, Ellen?"

Ellen shook her head slowly.

"I won't give you away."

"Thank you," Stewart said, as she started to turn away. "You do know the risks. I mean if General Graycliffe..."

"Let's just pretend you never spoke to me," Ellen suggested.

Stewart nodded solemnly.

.14.

Uniformed security guards peered into the green station wagon as Joyce, Andy and Turtle pulled up to the TASCOM security gate.

The guards waved them through into the security tunnel. Andy parked the car and they were escorted into a long, narrow corridor. They stayed close together, each looking around suspiciously.

"This must be a nightmare for him," Joyce said, squeezing Andy's hand tightly.

As they walked down the hall, Dr. Stewart suddenly stepped forward from a side room to greet them. Andy automatically shook the doctor's hand.

"Welcome to TASCOM, all of you," Dr. Stewart said with sincerity.

"Dr. Stewart, what is this place?" Andy asked, getting to the point.

"You said we could see Daryl. Is he all right?" Turtle asked nervously.

Joyce had not let go of Andy's hand. She looked toward Stewart with pain in her eyes. "Can we see him, please?"

Without replying, Dr. Stewart crossed to a door, opened it and stood back to allow the visitors to precede him inside.

They entered the computer room. The acronym D.A.R.Y.L. was embossed over the rows of humming machines. The Richardsons and Turtle looked around hesitantly, not sure of what they were looking at.

Dr. Stewart was uncertain about how to break the news to them gently.

"What is this?" Andy demanded.

They stared around in complete incomprehension. Joyce shuddered and moved closer to Andy.

Dr. Stewart took a deep breath.

"Daryl is not—never was—completely human," he blurted out.

The three of them stood motionless, not understanding the meaning of his words.

Andy looked blank. "What is this," he asked angrily, "a bad joke?"

Stewart pointed up toward the acronym on the wall. "Data-Analyzing Robot Youth Life-form. Daryl," he said. "Daryl is an experiment in artificial intelligence."

Unconsciously, Joyce began to shake her head,

denying an idea she could not handle. "No, no, it's not true!" she mumbled. "No, no..."

Dr. Stewart paused and looked at the three startled people. "Believe me, I know what you must feel. All I can say is...he was never meant to be... with people like yourselves."

Turtle looked around in silent wonderment at the hardware surrounding them. He grasped the idea faster than the adults as he recalled some of Daryl's extraordinary abilities.

"Holy shit," Turtle whispered. "He's a robot!"

"Well, he's more than that, Turtle, a lot more," Dr. Stewart explained. "This is where we program the computer in Daryl's head—and where he discharges learned information in the mainframe memory."

"Oh, wow!" Turtle exclaimed.

Joyce just shook her head and shivered. "I don't believe this."

Dr. Stewart walked over to a keyboard, distressed at his own inability to break this news gently. "I can understand that you wouldn't, Mrs. Richardson," he said. He rested his hand on the computer keyboard. "Look, ask this computer any detail, no matter how small, ask it something that could only be known to you and Daryl."

"Is this some kind of a joke?" Joyce cried.

Dr. Stewart shook his head. "I'm afraid not." His fingers flew over the keys and he tilted the computer screen toward them: HI, DARYL. TURTLE IS HERE

AND WANTS TO KNOW IF THIS IS REALLY YOU.

Immediately a response appeared: HI, TURTLE.

There was a pause. Then the screen read: I STILL DON'T KNOW—WHAT'S A HOOKER?

Breathless, Turtle turned to Stewart. "Okay, okay!" he cried. "It's him!"

Daryl sat in his igloo room playing a computer game, totally unaware of any outside activity.

As they approached the domelike room, however, Andy, Joyce and Turtle could see Daryl through a one-way light-conducting wall.

Andy stared at the boy he had come to love. "Doesn't he know we're here?" he asked Stewart.

"He can't see us."

"But I just talked to him!" Turtle shouted.

'No," Stewart explained, "you talked to his memory banks. That's separate."

Turtle stared at his friend in the room beyond, awed at the idea. "Daryl? A robot?"

Joyce was beside herself at this talk of robots and memory banks. "But he's...he's real! Look at him! He's just a little boy—flesh and blood." She stopped, horror-stricken at a horrible possibility, "Isn't he?"

"Not even a doctor could spot the differences," Stewart explained gently, "unless he X-rayed the skull. Daryl was not conceived in the womb, but in a laboratory test tube. With the computer brain provided by us. He's growing at a normal rate right now..."

Joyce closed her eyes and turned her face into Andy's shoulder, sickened.

"Buy why?" Andy asked. "Why all this?"

Carried away by his own enthusiasm, Dr. Stewart began a defense of the need to develop Daryl. "Why? Because the five senses of the human body are the fastest, most efficient method of programming ever devised. Imagine, sight, sound, touch, taste, smell...all that going for you, instead of just one guy punching keys at a computer terminal..."

The explanation failed to calm Joyce and Andy's fears. They huddled together anxiously with Dr. Stewart as Turtle had the first opportunity to visit with Daryl.

Turtle carefully and quietly descended narrow steps. At the bottom he came to a door. It was perfectly flush with the curving outer wall of Daryl's igloo. There was no handle. Turtle pushed a button. The door slid open.

Daryl was engrossed in the computer game when he suddenly felt he was being watched. He turned and his face lit up when he saw Turtle standing there.

Impulsively Daryl started toward his friend, but stopped suddenly. It was obvious that both boys felt awkward about the reunion. They wanted to hug each other, but were unable to show their true emotion.

"Turtle!"

"Hi!"

"Oh, you came!" Daryl's eyes started to fill with tears. "With Mom...Joyce and Andy?"

"Sure, they're here but I gave them the slip,"

Turtle bragged. "They were listening to all the scientific crap about you." He approached Daryl more closely, circling him, eyeing him curiously.

"Did you know you were...you were a robot?"

"Well, I...I guess, uh, no. Not back home, with Andy and Joyce and you. I'd lost my memory—remember?"

"But now?" Turtle paused.

"Oh, now I remember."

Turtle was quiet for a moment, trying to decide what to ask. "How does it feel?"

Daryl shrugged. "It feels just the same."

"But do you feel like...I mean, like me?"

"I don't know." Daryl smiled. "I'm not you." He stopped for a moment and then added, "I think I feel like you. Why shouldn't I?"

The boys turned toward the door as they heard a sound. The Richardsons and Dr. Stewart entered, standing just inside the room. Daryl beamed with delight at this second treat in just a few moments.

"Oh, wow!" he cried as he spotted Joyce and Andy. He started to run toward them, but slowed to a stop when he saw the looks on their faces. Whatever it was frightened him. Joyce and Andy stood frozen. Neither came toward him. They stared at Daryl with a curious and almost terrified intensity.

The smile faded from Daryl's face.

"Mom? Dad?"

Joyce covered her face with her hands as a sob escaped her lips. She looked to Dr. Stewart and then to Andy for help. Neither spoke.

Then Andy, his gaze still frozen on Daryl, stepped hesitantly towards him.

"Daryl, I..." Andy bent down on one knee. His eyes were level with Daryl's. "I guess it wasn't my coaching that was going to put you in the Hall of Fame. You had the stuff all by yourself, huh?" He smiled.

Daryl and Andy stared into each other's eyes and the fears disappeared.

"It's great to see you, kid," Andy cried, pulling the boy to his chest.

Daryl held his arms around Andy's neck and looked over toward Joyce. He let go of Andy and, arms outstretched, ran to the only mother he had ever known. Joyce ran to the boy as she burst into tears.

She picked him up and held him so tight he was soon sputtering for breath. Soon both were laughing and crying, happy to be together again.

In too short a time the visit was over. Dr. Stewart escorted the Richardsons and Turtle through the security area. They spoke quietly, the Richardsons nodding their heads while Stewart gestured for silence.

"Are you sure?" Stewart asked.

"Oh, yes," Joyce answered. "We're sure."

"And remember, Turtle," the doctor reminded, "you don't talk to anyone."

Turtle mimed a zipper across his lips. Joyce smiled broadly and impulsively kissed Dr. Stewart before jumping into the car.

.15.

The Richardson visit seemed to go off without a hitch. The family left and Daryl remained in his igloo, returning to complete his computer game.

Dr. Stewart walked with Ellen along a glass-lined corridor in the research center. Lights started to flicker on throughout the building as it became dark outside.

All of a sudden they heard a noise in the distance.

"What could that be?" Stewart asked, as they walked toward a door.

Outside they watched a convoy of military vehicles with motorcycle escorts approach TASCOM and surround the building.

General Graycliffe walked from the large staff car, followed by his assistant, Major Williams, and strode through the main entrance.

At the door, Stewart was confronted by the general and Major Williams.

Ellen stood just inside the door, separated from the three men.

Turning toward her, General Graycliffe said, "You did the right thing, calling us, Dr. Lamb."

Stewart shot her an accusing glance as Ellen sheepishly looked to the floor.

"I'm not putting you under arrest, Dr. Stewart," the general said.

"Since you've sealed off the whole building, that's hardly a big concession, General," Stewart replied.

The general silenced him with a glance. "What in the name of hell were you trying to *do?*"

"I told you," Stewart maintained. "I believe Daryl is more than a machine. We've created something we have no right to destroy."

"Dr. Lamb," the general said, turning to Ellen, "as a scientist, do you share this view?"

"No," Ellen answered. "Dr. Stewart is falling into the same trap that Dr. Mulligan did. Attributing human emotion where none exists. It cannot exist in a machine."

Stewart interrupted, visibly angry. "He is *not* a machine."

"Nobody believes that except you, Stewart," Graycliffe said.

"The Richardsons believe it," the doctor replied.

"Oh, the Richardsons. Forget them!" The general dismissed the suggestion.

His emotion building, Stewart stared straight at the general.

"You are asking us to *kill* a child. The body is organic. It will hurt, die, decompose, just like you and me, General. This is not a piece of scrap metal to send to the junkyard. This is a boy!"

Stewart looked pleadingly to Ellen for a response. She looked away.

"Dr. Lamb," the general asked, "can you dispose of this prototype?"

She hesitated. "There would be a loss of valuable data. We're still learning aspects we hadn't ...," she faltered.

The general interrupted, turning to Stewart. "You have the paperwork which notifies you of our requirements for the next generation."

Stewart slumped in defeat as the general glared at him.

"I am relying upon you to inform me when the disposal is completed, Dr. Stewart. Or shall I look to Dr. Lamb for that?"

Dr. Stewart gave the general a reluctant shake of the head and then turned to Dr. Lamb.

General Graycliffe and Major Williams watched silently as the two doctors left the room and headed down the corridor to the D.A.R.Y.L. headquarters. Neither spoke. Dr. Stewart began issuing orders into the computer keyboard.

Dr. Lamb pressed buttons summoning clinical assistants to the area. Within moments, the operating theater was bustling with quiet but determined activity.

Still sleeping, Daryl had been moved from his igloo room into the center of the operating room.

Asleep throughout most of the preparation, he awakened suddenly. Staring at something directly above him, he screamed in terror.

A mask covered Dr. Lamb's face as she stared down at the hysterical child who was strapped to the bed.

The scientists stood around the bed in silence, trying to tune out the screams. Suddenly there was silence.

Dr. Stewart and Dr. Lamb walked from the operating room to the outside corridor, removing their rubber gloves and surgeon's gowns. There was a hostile silence between them as General Graycliffe approached.

"It's over. I hope you're both satisfied," Stewart said harshly, looking toward the general. Dark rings stood out beneath his eyes. In just a few hours, the doctor seemed to have aged years. He stalked off in the opposite direction, leaving the general and Ellen Lamb behind.

Graycliffe then proceeded into the operating room and looked around. A tray of used surgical instruments stood next to the operating table. A child-sized gown lay crumpled on the floor. Dr. Lamb watched from the doorway.

Two attendants entered from another door, pushing a trolley with a huge bag for used linen.

Graycliffe turned his attention to a computer terminal alongside the operating table. He punched several keys. The screen read: PROJECT D.A.R.Y.L.

He hit a few more keys and a mass of data rolled up on the screen. He pressed two more keys. LIFE-FORM TERMINATED, the screen read. ORGANIC SECTOR TERMINATED.

As the general continued his follow-up on the termination of D.A.R.Y.L., Dr. Stewart headed out of the TASCOM building. He got into his station wagon and drove toward the gate, now manned by armed soldiers.

One soldier walked slowly around the vehicle. He peered in. Stewart was alone. Nothing seemed amiss. A second soldier was on the gatehouse telephone. His glance toward Stewart made it clear that the doctor was the subject of the conversation.

At the same time, Graycliffe went into the computer room to read a printout of the Daryl material. The papers clattered out of the machine, passing through his hands and into a pile in a wire tray.

A bank of computer screens surrounding him also displayed the information—TERMINATED—but Graycliffe did not look at these.

When the printout was completed, Graycliffe hit two keys to close the machine down. He looked down at the sheaf of papers as the computer screen message changed suddenly.

I HOPE WE GET AWAY WITH THIS! Half-looking at

the screen, Graycliffe switched it off. As he did, the words caught his eye and he lunged to bring the screen up again. He turned the switch back on, but the screen was blank. Grabbing the printout of what had appeared on the screen, he scanned the papers furiously, and ran from the computer room into the operating theater.

Ellen Lamb was still cleaning up as Graycliffe rushed in and pulled open a thick glass door set in the wall.

"Sonofabitch! First Mulligan, then Stewart, now you. Why?" he screamed at her as she stood frozen across the room.

The general ran and grabbed the nearest phone, swinging around to face Ellen.

In a surprisingly calm voice she replied, "General, a machine becomes human when you can't tell the difference anymore."

He stared at her briefly, as if admitting what she said might be true. But he quickly became a general again when the phone was answered at the other end.

"Get me the gate!" he said with quiet menace.

The phone rang in the security gatehouse as the gates closed behind Dr. Stewart's station wagon, which drove into the night.

The rear seat heaved and bucked from pressure underneath.

"We made it! Can I come out now? It's hot in here," Daryl called to the doctor in the front.

"Hold it," Stewart warned. "We're not clear yet."

But Daryl's head had already emerged, his face split from ear to ear by a happy grin of triumph.

When the phone was finally answered at the gatehouse, Dr. Stewart was miles down the road and out of sight.

In the wake of his exit, a full-scale alert was called, and soldiers piled into waiting vehicles for the chase.

The station wagon traveled along the dark road, Daryl sat up alongside Stewart now, peering out the back window for signs of the pursuing soldiers.

Suddenly the lights of the military convoy came into view.

"I can see them!" Daryl cried out.

"Okay, fasten your seat belt," Stewart ordered.

He swung the car off the main road and onto a steep, rough track, killing the lights. As the car bucked and bounced painfully, Stewart squinted hard to see where he was driving in the dark.

Daryl peered through the windshield, trying to help guide the bouncing vehicle. "Watch out for that rock—go left," he called.

Stewart swung the wheel, moving the car along the dark, rocky path.

In the distance, Daryl and Stewart could hear the engines of dozens of pursuing cars, and trucks tearing past them. No one had even noticed the road taken by the doctor and the boy.

Military helicopters, police patrol cars and police helicopters were ordered to join the chase as the station wagon continued its escape.

Stewart's car slithered down a dusty slope. It

reached the bottom of the slope, narrowly missing a couple of nearby shacks. Stewart fought the wheel, trying to retain control as the car rocked and bumped its way onto a side road.

Daryl wiped his mouth nervously and looked over at Stewart. The doctor peered intently into the darkness.

"Better use your lights now or we'll look suspicious," Daryl suggested.

"Good thinking," Stewart said, switching on the headlights.

"You want me to drive?" Daryl asked.

"No. You'd attract too much attention."

Daryl shrugged, not really understanding. He looked out the window and saw the next sign which read: FREEWAY ENTRANCE ½ MI. They drove in silence for a moment.

The whoop of a police siren screamed with sickening suddenness. Lights flashed behind them, moments later beside them. They were flanked by moving police cars. The police held up their weapons.

"Pull it over, Doctor," a policeman yelled over his bullhorn.

Stewart groaned in despair.

"Turn onto the freeway, quick," Daryl ordered.

"Huh?" Stewart looked blankly at the boy.

"Take the freeway! It's our only chance."

Police cars signaled Stewart to slow down. The station wagon was on the inside lane, and other than shooting them, the police could not stop the vehicle.

Just then, one police car moved ahead to make a barrier in front of Stewart's car.

Stewart took Daryl's advice. He jerked the wheel as the wagon screamed up the ramp and onto the freeway.

The knot of police cars followed up the ramp, their sirens shrieking in the night.

The chase was on!

Stewart squeezed the wagon in and out of heavy traffic and accelerated. Daryl looked back. Four, five, six, at least ten police cars were behind them!

Daryl slid next to Stewart until they were shoulder to shoulder. Daryl's hands clutched at the wheel.

"We seem to have attracted attention, anyway." He grinned up at Stewart, who drove on grimly. "You've got to trust me now. Please, trust me," he begged.

Stewart looked at the boy and shook his head. He lifted him over his lap to take the place behind the wheel, narrowly avoiding a collision with a truck to his right.

Other traffic moved aside as the police cars continued their hot pursuit, closing in on the station wagon. They were only twenty yards behind as Daryl took control of the driving.

"We can never outrun them," Stewart said.

"Why don't you, uh, close your eyes," Daryl said to the doctor. "And fasten your seat belt."

"Oh God. What are you going to do, Daryl?"

"It's okay," Daryl reassured him, thinking of his first round of Pole Position. "I've done it before."

Daryl was calm. He jerked the wheel, first to the right, then left, left again, right. With incredible precision and absolute confidence, he played Pole Position on the freeway.

The flow of traffic on the freeway slowed down as it funneled into two lanes for some construction work ahead. Despite his extraordinary driving, Daryl found himself wedged between the slowing vehicles ahead and the relentless police cars.

He noticed a tow truck to his left. Suddenly, he drove the front wheel of Stewart's car onto the hood of the car in tow and literally skied his car through the narrow gaps in the traffic.

Eventually Daryl found his way cleared, but two police cars had managed to squeeze through and moved to block him as he landed back on four wheels.

"Daryl," Stewart gasped, "look out!" The car headed straight for the construction area and the freeway center divider. Suddenly the three cars leaped over the center divider, narrowly missing the oncoming traffic. Both police cars turned over.

Incredibly, the officers climbed out of the totaled vehicles and looked after the flying station wagon, as Daryl headed up the wrong side of the freeway.

"Oh my God," Stewart howled, as he slammed

on his seat belt and slid down in the seat. "I can't look!"

Horns screamed and lights blazed as Daryl's amazing reflexes kept Stewart's car intact, avoiding near misses with almost every turn.

The police stared in wonder and frustration as they kept level with Daryl in the opposite lane.

"You seem to be enjoying this, Daryl," Stewart observed, looking up at the boy.

Daryl did not respond. He was almost relaxed as he flicked the car in and out, now weaving a steady pattern between the never-ending stream of approaching vehicles. He was absolutely sure of his ability, even at this high speed.

Dr. Stewart kept his eyes shut tight, clutching the car seat for dear life. He occasionally peeped out the windshield, only to be terrified sufficiently to pull him back out of sight again.

Daryl moved the car away from the center divider. The police cars, still traveling level with him, were in the normal lane.

Suddenly an access ramp loomed in the lane where Daryl was driving the wrong way. Daryl whipped the car over and headed down the ramp, moving rapidly away from the police, who were now stranded on the wrong side of the freeway with no matching exit.

"All right!" Daryl said triumphantly as he lurched off the exit amid a blare of horns. He crossed the approach road and headed down another highway, this time traveling in the right direction.

Dr. Stewart finally emerged from the floor and blinked in admiration at the boy beside him.

"Round one to science," the doctor sighed.

.16.

The car plodded down the highway, heading farther into the rugged countryside. Old worn-down houses bordered by jagged wire fences skirted the road. A few cows stood lazily in the pastures. Thin horses nuzzled at the skimpy grasslands.

Stewart slumped asleep on the car seat as Daryl drove. The boy glanced occasionally at the dipping gas gauge. Night had slowly turned to dawn and the sun was rising brilliantly ahead on the roadway. The car suddenly started jerking and sputtering. The movement awakened Stewart, who stretched from his uncomfortable position. He looked at Daryl.

"Must have konked out." He smiled sheepishly at the ten-year-old boy who confidently held the wheel. "I wonder where we are?"

"It's not where we are but how we're going to get where we want to go," Daryl said, pointing down to the nearly empty gauge.

For the last few miles the car had been riding mostly on hope. The gauge now read empty. The car sputtered again, giving a last gasp of gas-fed life, and halted as Daryl steered it slowly onto the side of the roadway.

Daryl and Stewart looked around at the sparse countryside. It spoke of poverty, but underneath it all projected a sense of beauty and pride. They both sighed and looked at each other.

Up ahead they noticed a tumbledown farmhouse. Parked nearby was a battered pickup truck. There was no one in sight.

"Let's check out the farmhouse," Stewart suggested.

The pair got out of the car and pushed it a short distance down the road to the farm gate.

The house, white clapboard with black shutters, stood somewhat back from the gate. In front was a series of outbuildings—barn, silo and workshed. All were badly in need of painting.

Stewart walked over to the pickup truck. He checked it over.

"No one seems to be here to need it," Daryl said with a mischievous grin.

He and Stewart exchanged a "why not?" glance.

Moments later Stewart was under the hood, hot-wiring the vehicle.

"Look in the glove compartment of the car," Stewart told Daryl, handing him a ten-dollar bill. "There's paper and pencil. Just say, 'The car's yours and sorry for the trouble and here's ten dollars for the gas.'"

Daryl started writing. Stewart got behind the wheel.

The pickup truck lumbered onto the highway, wheezing and wobbling.

"That guy got one helluva good deal," Stewart said of the trade.

The truck coughed along. No sooner had it started moving steadily down the road, than Daryl quickly ducked down in the passenger seat out of sight.

A police car whizzed past them, barely noticing the driver of the ancient vehicle.

As the escapees continued their flight, General Graycliffe sat alert but indignant in his office, looking for answers to the question of the disappearance. "I refuse to believe they can just...disappear," the disgruntled general scowled at the three men who sat in his office.

"They can't, General," the colonel answered, "but we're spread thin. When we sight them, we'll get them."

The general sipped his coffee, only somewhat mollified.

◻ ◻ ◻

Daryl pulled up from under the front seat and breathed a sigh of relief. Stewart drove and Daryl sat up in the passenger seat, his eyes darting from the front to the back windows as a lookout. After a few miles, his tension eased and he gazed at the countryside surrounding them. The highway bent around a craggy mountain and extended in a long steady curve toward the plains beyond.

Daryl peered down into the valley as the truck continued on a roller-coaster cruise along the highway. Sprawling as far as his eye could see were patches of farmland, stretching wide and open to the foot of the mountain range just beyond. Daryl's thoughts drifted as his mind took in the beauty of the countryside.

"Oh, oh," he said suddenly, breaking the serene silence.

"What is it?" Stewart asked anxiously.

"There's a roadblock ahead."

"Where?" Stewart asked, squinting his eyes and peering through the windshield.

"A way down, about two miles," Daryl answered, deep in concentration. "Only one car and one cop, though."

"It's enough," Stewart said glumly, as they headed toward the unavoidable roadblock.

The trooper stood alongside his black and white cruiser, which was parked across the country road. Two cones blocked the other side of the road.

"Check back, buddy, okay? Over and out," he

called into his radio microphone. The trooper placed the mike back inside the cruiser just as the old pickup crested the rise in the hill. The truck slowed to a halt about twenty yards from the barrier.

The sun shone brightly behind the truck. As he approached the vehicle, the trooper reached into his pocket and took out a pair of sunglasses. He dropped the shades over his eyes and, with his rifle cradled in his arm, ambled toward the old farmer sitting in the cab.

As the trooper walked toward the truck, Daryl emerged from bushes behind his back and made his way toward the parked cruiser.

Glancing into the cab of the truck, the trooper eyed the grimy old farmer sitting alone behind the wheel.

"Howdy. What's up?" Stewart asked the trooper in his best country twang.

"Howdy," the trooper answered, looking into the cab. "Nothin' much."

Stewart glanced past the trooper to check on Daryl, who had reached the parked police car and was already busy at work.

Quickly and systematically, Daryl's fingers felt for the fuse box under the dashboard. Then, like a pianist running up the keyboard with one finger, he dislodged and pocketed all the fuses.

"Checkin' for a coupla runaways," the trooper explained, about to dismiss the straggly old farmer who did not meet the description. "Well..." he seemed about to wave Stewart on and return to his car.

Looking to buy some time for Daryl to complete the sabotage, Stewart called out to the trooper. "Trouble ya for a light? I'm out." He held up a cigarette from an old pack on the dashboard of the truck.

"Back in my car," the trooper said, turning toward the cruiser as if to oblige the request.

Quickly, Stewart called out again, causing the trooper to turn back toward the pickup. "Nah, forget it. Gotta quit anyhow." He laughed.

Crouched below the dash of the police car, Daryl had finished his sabotage. He ran quickly back into the bushes and headed down the road. Stewart saw his signal to start rolling again.

He waved a friendly farewell to the lone trooper. "Okay, thanks. See ya," he called as he drove off.

"Drive safe," the trooper called back. He walked to the other side of the road, lifted the two cones aside and waved Stewart on to pass. Just as he replaced them on the asphalt, he looked up in time to see Stewart slow the truck down and pick up Daryl who hopped in from the roadside.

"Hey!" the trooper called after the fleeing truck, which sped away with its brakes screeching.

The trooper jumped behind the wheel of his car and reached for the keys. "Shit!" he screamed, realizing that the keys had disappeared.

Reaching for the radio, he groaned. The microphone had mysteriously disappeared, just like the keys.

"Shit!" he yelled again, leaping out of the car, rifle in hand. He fired wild shots into the air after the truck.

Stewart and Daryl smiled jubilantly at each other. "You're getting to be some escape artist," Stewart complimented the boy. "That was great!"

"We're a pretty good team." Daryl returned the compliment, holding up the keys, microphone and fuses. "Not bad, huh?"

"You did great," Stewart said, smiling. He glanced in the rearview mirror at the figure of the fast-disappearing trooper, now stranded in the middle of nowhere. He was still firing wild shots into the air.

"I hope he had breakfast," Stewart chuckled.

As they swung around a corner, their delight suddenly turned to horror.

Standing in the middle of the road was a second trooper, his large rifle aimed at the oncoming pickup.

"Oh my God," Stewart cried. "That's why he fired shots. To tell this guy we were coming." They noticed a black and white police car concealed in the bushes as they headed into the ambush.

"Down!" Stewart shrieked, grabbing Daryl and pushing him to the floor of the cab. At the same instant, a rifle shot blasted through the windshield, shattering it completely.

Clutching the steering wheel tightly, Stewart

fishtailed the truck wildly, forcing the trooper to leap for safety before he could manage a second shot at the fugitives. The truck slammed into the front of the hidden police car, crushing its front end.

"Stay down," Stewart hissed to the terrified Daryl, as he punched what was left of the glass out of the windshield. He struggled with the gears and slammed the accelerator to the floor.

The trooper steadied himself to get off another series of shots, but the truck's rear wheels spun with such force that a shower of stones and gravel blinded him, forcing him to turn away and shield his eyes.

The old truck lurched out of sight. Before the trooper managed to ready his gun, the truck was gone. He ran to his car and spotted the damage. "Damn," he shouted, reaching for the radio inside his car and calling to police headquarters.

"Headquarters, this is Car Twenty-two. Come in, please."

"I think we made it," Daryl said shakily, crawling back onto the seat alongside Stewart.

The doctor did not answer as he fought with the wheel of the truck, wrestling the speeding vehicle through a long corner.

Hearing no answer, Daryl turned to the driver. He froze in horror. "You've been shot! Oh, Dr. Stewart, you're hurt," Daryl cried.

A huge patch of blood spread over Stewart's shirt

from a massive bullet wound to the side of his chest. His face was contorted with pain.

"That was the bullet that would have shot me," Daryl cried, climbing over the man and taking the wheel of the speeding truck. "They're really after me. Move over here," he ordered. "I'll find some place to stop."

.17.

News of the roadblock incident had yet to reach officials, but the war room was already in action. Illuminated only somewhat by huge lit-up wall maps, the dim room was highlighted with flashing computer screens as panels furiously spit out print-outs.

General Graycliffe entered the immense center and strode to the middle of the room, where shirt-sleeved aides were overseeing the incoming data. An aide entered, breathless. "They ran a roadblock, sir," he informed the stern-faced general. "Kyle County."

"Dammit, Major," the general reprimanded without slowing his stride, "if it was a proper roadblock nobody should have crashed it. Least of all Stewart and that...child."

Looking blank, the aide responded, "Yes, sir."

"I want a full report," the general ordered.

"Yes, sir."

The general swept down into the center of this massive control zone, headquarters of the power of the United States military. He warned all in the room, "These two must be caught or killed before they start running to some busybody from the press."

As the hunt intensified, Daryl took the wheel from the bleeding scientist and guided the old truck deep into a wooded glade. The boy's eyes were filled with tears.

Stewart lay in a thicket of woods, a beautiful clearing where the fading light of day threw long, deep shadows over the green natural landscape. His face was gray, contorted with pain. "I'm sorry, Daryl," Stewart said sadly.

"If I was older, you could have given me a medical program; I could go to medical school...and...that'd be helpful, I mean for more than just helping you..."

Stewart squeezed the boy's hand. "They'll go on hunting you, Daryl," he warned, his breath coming with more difficulty. "Hunting until they've killed you."

"Or," Daryl mused, "until they *think* they have."

Stewart didn't hear this last thought. He was sinking fast. "What have I done?" Stewart moaned, as if in confession. "Made you a fugitive. Frightened you. Lied to you. Taken you from the only love you ever found..."

Daryl held the dying man's head in his lap, consoling him. "You *gave* me everything, too," he whispered softly, gently. "I mean being...a real human."

Stewart looked up at the child's simple face, filled with intensity and anguish. He reached out and touched his cheek, as a father would touch his son in valediction. He softly brushed the tears that ran down Daryl's face.

"Daryl," Stewart said, having difficulty in getting out the words. "I want you to remember always, always, what I'm telling you now." He forced the pain out of his eyes for an instant. "You are...a real person. You...are real. I just wish..." He fought for breath. "Wish I could see...how it all worked out for you. But don't doubt it. Never."

With a final sigh, Stewart turned on his side and died.

Daryl checked his pulse. He looked at the dead man's eyelids. The blood-soaked, bullet-torn shirt was the only confirmation anyone needed that Dr. Jeffrey Stewart was dead.

Tears filled Daryl's eyes as he leaned down and kissed Stewart on the forehead. He stared at the man who had become his friend. Then he sat back a moment and gazed up at the darkening skies. Suddenly, deep and low in the empty night came the sound of heartbreaking sobs...that could only have been made by a real person.

.18.

Daryl covered Stewart's body with the doctor's torn jacket and started to make his way into the woods. He turned for a final look at the man who had risked his life for Daryl.

He climbed back into the broken-down truck and headed toward a side road, driving almost instinctively toward his objective. Seeing headlights in the distance, he abandoned the truck in the woods and proceeded on foot.

It was very dark. The night hung heavy with expectation. Daryl felt his heart pounding in anticipation, but determination overpowered his fear. He ducked as he spotted the headlights of a jeep. Daryl hid in a thicket and watched as military police swept the jeep around in an arc. Turning by a shed, the jeep headed back in the direction from which it had come.

The headlights had missed their target. Daryl was already three-quarters of the way up the fence, clinging like an angry spider. He stared into the darkness, his face lined with deep fury and certainty, a look of intensity he had never displayed before.

In three swift movements, Daryl was over the top of the fence. He dropped to the ground inside the perimeter of the military base.

He stood and walked forward, filled with confidence. Moments later, he stopped suddenly, his legs barely two inches from a trip wire. Daryl stepped over the wire and continued his advance.

Daryl made out a group of buildings and some airplanes in the distance. He noticed a handful of dim lights, a maintenance squad and some military activity.

Inside the control tower, technicians manned a console which indicated a large plan of the base, with winking lights pinpointing deployment of patrols and aircraft.

Daryl slid closer to the military structure and stood flat against the outside brick wall. Steel doors led into storerooms. He peered inside at his target: an object about the size of a vending machine, with a TV screen and a red phone attached, as well as a computer keyboard.

The sign above the keyboard and machine read: FIRE COMMAND POST. Daryl quickly entered the building, walked down the hall unnoticed and took his place in front of the machine.

He carefully levered open the plate-glass door covering the machine. Silence. Daryl heaved a sigh of relief—no directly wired alarms, he thought thankfully. Fingers flying, he went to work on the keyboard.

A technician sitting in the tower with several computer screens around him felt the results of Daryl's efforts. Suddenly he realized that something odd was happening on the screen in front of him. "Hold on," he called. "I've got a fire alert here."

Figures began flashing up at random on the screen.

"Jesus! I've got them everywhere!" the technician shrieked.

Daryl remained at the fire command console, still zapping away at the simple keyboard. The screen in front of him flashed all kinds of codes, including the words RESTRICTED ACCESS. Each time this code came up, Daryl knew exactly how to break the code so the screen yielded its secrets.

Suddenly the control tower instruments went completely out of control. "Something really crazy is happening . . . ," the technician said, looking around in confusion. The computer screens lining the room started flickering and rolling numbers in a blinding blur of speed, faster than the eyes could read them.

"What in hell's . . . ?" The technician scratched his head.

"Oh my God," a second technician yelped as he

came into the room. "All the power circuits are going crazy!"

Still in the corridor, Daryl continued zapping away on the fire command console. Suddenly hearing a sound, he turned swiftly. Two soldiers stared dumbfounded at him from the far end of the corridor.

"It's a kid!" one of the soldiers said.

"No, it's *the* kid!" the other yelled, breaking into a run toward Daryl.

Spotting his pursuers, Daryl lunged for the light switch on the wall. At once the hall was black.

Daryl moved silently away from the scuffling noises.

"Shit!" one soldier screamed, obviously hitting the wall. When he finally reached a light switch, the hall was illuminated, but Daryl was gone.

In the darkness, Daryl had raced out a side door to what he found to be the fighter airbase. He crossed the wide concrete strip, which he realized was a runway.

Quickly night turned to day as every light on the runway was turned on. The blaze of light flared up into the night sky. Daryl hid in the shadows and walked on.

The cover of night was broken. Arc lamps burst on around the airbase. Searchlights stabbed the sky, scanning the field in relentless pursuit of their target.

Taut with emotion, anger and determination,

Daryl walked heedlessly across the field. His handiwork with the control console had thrown the tower into mass confusion.

"The circuits are completely screwed up! Every time I hit a switch I'm getting the late show," the technician mumbled, frantically hitting switches. He continued struggling in vain.

Out on the airbase field, Daryl walked with fearless certainty, unseen by the frustrated guards and military police who ran frantically around him. He marched on, beneath the military planes silhouetted against the sky. Nothing could stop him from achieving his goal, for himself and as a memorial to Dr. Stewart.

Suddenly, through the noise of the chaos came the distant roar of an engine. At first the military men did not notice it in the general turmoil. Gradually the officers and men peered around in search of the source of the ever-increasing sound.

Then two officers posted on the field spotted it: a sleek black fighter plane taxiing down the illuminated runway.

The enraged controllers in the tower could not communicate with the airplane. The center of attention turned to the airfield where men, in and out of uniform, ran toward the black jet which moved confidently toward a take-off position.

For a moment the bright lights focused on the pilot in the cockpit. Illuminated against the night sky, confident and smiling, sat Daryl, about to fly the Air Force's most frightening machine!

There was a roar of engines and the airplane moved even faster toward vector speed. Hurtling down the runway, it lifted into the night sky where it was almost instantly swallowed up by darkness. Daryl's lesson on his plane ride from Barkenton to TASCOM headquarters had paid off.

Down below, hundreds of military men and government agents waved frantically and uselessly as the plane sped away into the night. As they stood on the field, the lights suddenly began to fade and switch off, as if the source of power had mysteriously withdrawn.

Daryl's flight enraged the top brass of the military, bringing them to the war room where his inflight actions were monitored on a huge TV screen. The screen received transmissions from a remote TV camera inside the cockpit of the military jet, where the furious and embarrassed generals saw Daryl jubilantly flying one of the most expensive airplanes in United States military history.

As the monitor showed the back of Daryl's head and the state-of-the-art instrumentation panel at his fingertips, a tracking map of the southeastern United States seaboard tracked the movement of the plane.

An Air Force general had been rushed to the scene when news of Daryl's escape was learned. "I'm sorry, but if that plane leaves United States airspace we've no choice," the general told Graycliffe, who stared in disbelief.

"You mean you're going to shoot it down?" Gray-cliffe asked in astonishment.

"We can't do that," the Air Force general laughed bleakly. "There isn't a missile built that's fast enough to catch it." Looking up at the display monitor that indicated the plane's cockpit and instrument panel, he added, "Trouble is, there is far too much technology up there that we cannot let fall into the wrong hands."

"So what are you going to do?" Graycliffe asked.

Looking both proud and ashamed, the Air Force general outlined the alternative. "Our contingency planners thought ahead—to some such almighty foul-up as this. We did the only thing possible—built an explosive charge into the plane itself. If there's no other way of stopping it, I push this little button right here," he said, pointing to a small black switch, "and it explodes instantly, wherever it is."

Graycliffe looked up slowly to meet the man's gaze. "Well, now...," Graycliffe almost smiled, "that might solve a whole score of problems."

"Rightly so," the general agreed, "but it's one hell of an expensive way to do it!"

As the generals determined his fate, Daryl took full control of the mighty Air Force weapon jet, enjoying every moment of it. Relaxed and confident, he took a stick of gum from his pocket and chewed happily, keeping a close eye on the control panel. The speed indicator showed the plane flying at Mach 2.2—more than twice the speed of sound. The sensation was phenomenal.

Daryl dipped the plane down until he was flying barely five hundred feet above ground level, a soaring blackbird nearly slicing the peaks off mountaintops, traveling at a tremendous speed. Daryl scanned a map on the control panel and found Barkenton clearly marked. He then inserted the grid reference from the map into the computer and flicked the switch from manual to auto pilot. Now he could relax.

The plane continued its flight of fantasy without Daryl's guidance. In an effort to make radio contact with Daryl, a stream of communication had been constantly coming over the radio, amplified while Daryl did his tricks. Daryl had tuned out the warnings by placing the unit on a low volume, but now he switched it up to see what these folks were up to and grabbed for the radio mike.

As he tuned in, a voice over the radio boomed, "...within the next seven minutes. I repeat this warning. You leave United States airspace in six minutes and thirty seconds, mark that from ...now."

The clock was set on 06.30. Daryl hit the switch to start the clock counting backwards. The radio warning continued. "Your aircraft will be destroyed if you do not turn around before that time. Please respond."

Daryl listened to the warning. He twisted knobs and waveband controls until the voice disappeared. A howl of other communication blasted over the speaker. Daryl played around with the switches un-

144

til he found the silent channel. The voices were stilled. He pressed a switch marked "Scramble." Then he picked up the microphone and called, "Hey CQ, this is your old pal QC. Will you wake up? This is QC calling CQ..."

Turtle was asleep but he stirred at the sound. The walkie-talkie crackled beside his head. He reached out to turn it off, fumbling instinctively. Suddenly, he recognized Daryl's voice, clear and distinct. Immediately he was wide awake. Turtle flung himself out of bed and scooped up the walkie-talkie.

"Daryl! Where are you?" Turtle called. "QC, come in, QC. I can hear you!"

Daryl touched the joystick and the airplane curved skyward like a rocket. He was in radio contact with Turtle! Grinning, Daryl called to his friend, "CQ, you wouldn't believe me if I told you!"

Standing impatiently behind a helpless technician at the control panel in the war room, the general shouted mercilessly at the young recruit.

"Well? What is he saying?" he bellowed, his face red with rage.

"He's scrambling," the anxious technician replied hesitantly.

"*Un*scramble it!" the general screamed.

"I'm trying, General, but..."

In the background, the general began pacing behind the helpless technician, muttering to himself.

□ □ □

The clock on the control panel had run down to four minutes to the threatened explosion when Daryl resumed his conversation with Turtle on the walkie-talkie.

"Listen," Daryl said, "I'll be home soon. Like Dr. Stewart promised. He's getting me home. Don't tell anybody. Okay? It's important."

"How soon is soon?" Turtle asked.

Checking the dials on the control panel, Daryl called back. "Less than twenty minutes? That's a guess, because the velocities are hard to calculate and the rates of descent are ..." He stopped the technical explanation.

"Meet me by Blue Lake before school."

"You got it!" Turtle called back jubilantly, muttering to himself as he jumped into his jeans and sweatshirt, "Velocities? ...Rates of descent? What is he up to now?"

Daryl focused the jet toward the mark for Barkenton on the computer grid. Suddenly the black airplane cut through a patch of the brightening dawn sky. As the plane curved around the horizon, Daryl glimpsed the sea off in the distance. The plane banked toward it. Looking ahead, Daryl prepared for his next move. He punched a new course into the plane's computer.

Back in the war room, General Graycliffe and the other observers intently watched the monitor image of Daryl programming the plane's computer. Suddenly Daryl took one hand from the control panel.

"What's he doing?" Graycliffe yelled, moving closer to view the image on the monitor.

"Get this."

The military experts watched open-mouthed as the ten-year-old boy took the gum he had been chewing and neatly stuck it over the mini–TV camera located behind his head. Suddenly the monitor which recorded the developments in the cockpit's interior went blank.

"A child with a stick of chewing gum has just rendered your hundred million dollars' worth of hardware useless," Graycliffe said icily to the silent technician. "Any suggestions?"

A doleful answer came from the Air Force general across the room.

"Looks like we're down to just the one, Lyford," he grimaced. He posed his hand on the "detonate" button. Seconds and minutes ticked off on the wall.

Far out in the dawning sky, Daryl grinned gleefully, setting his course on the computer. Finally, COURSE SET appeared on the screen, followed by AUTO. Daryl pressed another switch and a long series of figures reeled off the corner of a screen. The rest of the screen featured a computer-enhanced image of the ground ten miles below, whistling past at dizzying speed.

The airplane sped through the dawning sky, parallel to the coastline. Suddenly, it banked steeply, heading directly out toward the ocean. Inside the cockpit, Daryl's eyes flickered between the on-board computer screen and the clock, as he made a final complex calculation. With deliberation, he reached for a flap on the arm of his seat. Under the seat was a lever marked "Eject." His fingers hesitated momentarily on the lever. Then he bent to make one more final check.

Beside the ejector lever was a small recess labeled "Tracking Beacon—Automatic Activation." Daryl unlatched it quickly, removed two components and tossed them away. He turned to check the clock, counted off the last few seconds and pulled the lever.

In a flash, the ejector seat erupted from the cockpit, hurling its little bundle skywards. The plane continued on course.

The clock continued to click in the war room as both General Graycliffe and the Air Force general watched the countdown on the digital clock. The countdown to destruction of the jet was complete. Without hesitation, the Air Force general hit the switch with military precision.

The jet burst into flames, airwaves rocketing from the impact of the force. Daryl, inside the rocketing ejector seat, was already some miles clear when the plane exploded. Even so, the seat was jarred and sent spinning by the shock wave and intensity of the blast. Daryl held on for dear life, his face strained and agonized as he fought the gravity forces which pressed upon him.

The war room spectators watched the explosive action. The tracking screen showed the Lockheed blip vanish. The sounds they had been tracking ended abruptly, leaving the room in deafening silence.

Daryl sat completely unconscious in the ejector seat, carried by a huge black parachute which floated slowly downward as the first rays of sunshine broke on the horizon.

.19.

The alien silence of the war room took on new life as the sounds of various machines, satellite receivers, and sonar and radar screens reactivated.

"Target vaporized at 6:08, sir," a technician reported to the Air Force general.

The general, content with the report, peered over at a frowning General Graycliffe. "I think that concludes everything, Lyford," the general observed.

"He could have ejected," Graycliffe suggested.

The Air Force general smiled tolerantly. He checked with an operative who signaled that the Air Force general was correct. "We have a tracking signal on the ejector mechanism," the general explained. "We'd have picked it up instantly."

"I see," Graycliffe said quietly. "Well, thank you, gentlemen. And I'm sorry."

"About your prototype?"

"About your airplane," Graycliffe explained.

The two men looked bleakly at each other.

As Daryl hurtled through the sky, Turtle and Sherie Lee sneaked out of the house, jumped on their bicycles and pedaled out of town to meet Daryl. They headed toward the lake, the appointed meeting place. As they approached the familiar spot, they looked up to see the huge black parachute descending toward earth. Daryl, still unconscious, was strapped into the seat, blood streaming from his mouth. The chute continued its plunge toward earth, heading straight toward the water! The ejector seat holding Daryl plummeted like a stone, the black parachute spreading and settling on the water surface like a dark stain. Then, suddenly but slowly the parachute was sucked under by the weight of the chair and the child which it held. It disappeared completely beneath the surface with barely a ripple.

Even though he was unconscious, Daryl struggled for breath as the weight of the water and the parachute closed in around him. His fingers searched for the belt release, but could not find it. He struggled wildly, his eyes now opened wide in fear, but his wet fingers could not unloosen the unyielding belt.

Daryl struggled for his life beneath the surface of the water as Turtle and Sherie Lee approached the lake area on their bicycles. They looked around and saw nothing.

"So where is he?" Sherie Lee asked fearfully.

"I don't know," Turtle answered, looking around. "He said Blue Lake."

Daryl's hands moved convulsively under the water, without purpose. His eyes closed again. Daryl was dead. As life seemed to leave the organic body, the release mechanism opened on the seat, but the release came too late. The body floated upside down with the rest of the debris in the water.

Sherie Lee squinted her eyes as she peered out over Blue Lake. Suddenly she shrieked, pointing to the bunched-up little figure in the water. "Look!" she cried.

Turtle followed her gaze. Daryl's body floated in full view, face down, several yards down the shore of the lake.

"Oh, no...no, please," Sherie Lee cried. She lunged into the water tentatively. Turtle flung off his jacket and shoes and swam steadily toward the floating body. He grabbed the collar of Daryl's shirt and with agonizing slowness began to tow his friend toward shore. He called out to Sherie Lee, "Stop one of those cars up there. Hurry!!!"

Sherie Lee scrambled back to the mountain road and waved frantically.

Two cars and a truck screeched past the soaking-wet girl as she waved frantically from the roadside. Running into the middle of the road without any thought for her own life, Sherie Lee stumbled and held up her arms in command to the oncoming vehicle. The car stopped and pulled to the side of the road as Turtle struggled to bring himself and the lifeless body of his friend to shore.

The helpful driver loaded the two children and the lifeless Daryl into his car and sped them toward the hospital. But it was too late.

A swift team of physicians and nurses raced the boy onto a stretcher and into the emergency room. They drew the curtain around a small cubicle. Moments, which seemed like hours, passed. "I'm sorry," the doctor said to Turtle and Sherie Lee who waited clutching each other outside the cubicle. They were wrapped in blankets, teeth shivering, as Joyce, Andy, Howie and Elaine came running in.

Joyce collapsed with grief against Andy's shoulder. He led her gently from the room as Howie and Elaine looked on helplessly. Sherie Lee and Turtle, numb and red-eyed, stood up as the adults joined them. The group stood together, holding tightly to one another as if their physical closeness would prevent their emotional collapse.

Silently they squeezed into Howie's car in the parking lot. Elaine tried to comfort Turtle in the front while Sherie Lee, Joyce and Andy stared blankly into space in the backseat. As Howie drove the car from the parking lot, Joyce turned for a last look at her only son's final resting place . . . the hospital.

□ □ □

As the Foxes drove off, they didn't notice the woman sitting in a parked car across from the hospital. When the Fox's car had disappeared, she reached for a doctor's bag and made her way inside. All was quiet except for the clicking of her heels on the polished floor. The woman passed unnoticed through the corridor and silently slipped into Daryl's cubicle.

Once home, there were no words that anyone could offer as comfort.

"Dammit, Joyce, I want some answers!" Andy growled in anger, breaking the desperate silence.

She looked at him steadily, reminding him that answers would not return their son. Only miracles could do that.

Andy's outburst was followed by a single deep-throated sob from Turtle.

"It's okay to cry, Turtle," Sherie Lee said, touching her brother with affection and sympathy. "It's okay. You loved him."

But Turtle would not yet succumb. He struggled to come to terms with the notion at all. "He can't be dead! He *can't* be!" Turtle shouted, jumping up from his chair.

"I feel the same, Turtle, but there's nothing we can do," Sherie Lee consoled him.

"But he *can't* be!" Turtle insisted. "He's a robot! Robots don't die!"

"What do you mean?" she asked.

"Oxygen feeds your brain, but his brain is a microcomputer. That can't die. When you're dead, it means *brain death*!"

Everyone stared at him intently, slowly realizing what he was trying to say.

Knowing exactly what she had to do, the woman pulled back the sheet covering Daryl's body. "I know you can hear me, Daryl," Ellen Lamb said, as she took a small electrical device from her doctor's bag. "Everything's going to be all right," she assured him.

Daryl stood with Ellen Lamb outside the hospital, ready to return to his family. He reached toward her, grateful for the help she'd given him.

Ellen knew she should say something—perhaps wish him well—but she couldn't find the words to express what she was feeling. She met Daryl's hand briefly with her own, then quickly pulled away. But somehow Daryl was able to sense a bond between them.

Turning from her, he started to run, heading toward his family and friends as fast as his legs would carry him. He laughed, recognizing familiar places as he passed.

Turtle and Sherie Lee had just left the Richardson's house, tired and drained from their ordeal. Walking slowly down the street, Turtle squinted into the sunlight, unable to get a clear view of Daryl, who was running toward him. As Daryl moved closer, Turtle suddenly spotted his friend and ran to meet him, yelling, unable to believe his eyes.

Joyce and Andy, hearing the commotion, came from the house to see what was happening. Daryl and Turtle had come together in a fierce hug.

Laughter and tears mingled as Joyce and Andy joined the happy reunion. Their own little boy was home at last.